D0560124

PUBLIC LIBRARY WAYNE, N.J

FEB 0 2 2001

SISTER
HOOD

Sister Mary Teresa mysteries by Monica Quill

SISTER

HOOD

A SISTER MARY TERESA MYSTERY

Monica Quill

St. Martin's Press
New York

SISTER HOOD. Copyright © 1991 by Monica Quill. All rights reserved. Printed in the United States of America. No part of this book may be used or reproduced in any manner whatsoever without written permission except in the case of brief quotations embodied in critical articles or reviews. For information, address St. Martin's Press, 175 Fifth Avenue, New York, N.Y. 10010.

Design by Sharleen Smith

Library of Congress Cataloging-in-Publication Data

McInerny, Ralph M.
    Sister Hood / Monica Quill.
        p.   cm.
    ISBN 0-312-04602-2
    I. Title.
    PS3563.A31166S54   1991
    813'.54—dc20   90-27694
                        CIP

First Edition: August 1991
10 9 8 7 6 5 4 3 2 1

FOR DEBBIE AND FRED FREDDOSO

ONE

ONE

THE PASSENGERS DEPLANING at O'Hare came down the jetway into a waiting area full of people with expectant faces. There were cries of recognition, welcoming embraces, and here and there tears, whether of happiness or sorrow, it was difficult to say. All this hullabaloo was a matter of annoyance to business travelers, for whom a flight was simply a matter of getting from point A to point B. Salesmen who spent half their lives in the air were understandably impatient with passengers who acted as if the flight from St. Louis to Chicago rivaled the feats of Lindbergh and Amelia Earhart.

But after they pushed their way through the burbling relatives and reunited lovers there was a second team, unmistakably made up of reporters. Action cams were mounted on shoulders and TV interviewers, made-up and blow-dried, squinted with good-natured skepticism at some cosmic camera they imagined was always trained on them.

"That's her," someone yelled, and they surged forward, perhaps a dozen in all, an unstoppable phalanx.

Their target was a thin woman with high cheekbones and

slightly protruding eyes, completely undistinguished except for the small veil on her head.

"What's Chicago look like after all these years, Sister?" a reporter called, and the others chimed in.

"Are you here against your will?"

"Who's your lawyer?"

"Is it true you're doing penance for your whole family?"

The intensity and number of questions thrown at the nun made her the center of attention even for those who moments before had been absorbed in their own reunions. The bony religious stared openmouthed at the reporters, at the converging cameras, at the almost hostile questioners. Clearly she hadn't expected a reception like this.

"Were you subpoenaed, Sister?"

"I don't know what you're talking about." The nun spoke in a strangled voice.

Groans of disbelief.

"Who is she?" a salesman with BGB engraved on his briefcase asked a cameraman.

"The Moran daughter," a blond from Cable News said as she muscled past BGB toward the cornered nun.

"Aha."

The salesman turned to the person next to him to share this tidbit but was put off by the open-eyed innocence of the woman's gaze. She turned and started away from the gate, and BGB left too. It was the better part of valor to keep clear of such commotions. Besides, anything interesting would be on the TV news or in tomorrow morning's paper. He glanced at his watch, but it might have been a measure of the tension he was under rather than a need to know the time of day. He was always under tension, it went with the territory. He pressed his shoulder bag against his side and gripped its strap tightly.

BGB followed the signs to the baggage claim, with the wide-eyed woman to whom he had not spoken just ahead of him. Odd-looking bird. Her face put her in her thirties but her

4

thick black hair was pulled back and fastened in a bun and her outfit was that of an old woman—a bluish blouse buttoned to her throat, a black knit cardigan, and then the fullest skirt he had seen in years, heavy, woolen, a plaid in colors so dark the material seemed solid brown. Her shoes could have been a man's.

He plucked a cigarette from the pack in the pocket of his monogrammed shirt—BGB—and, still walking, carrying a briefcase as well as the shoulder bag, managed to light the cigarette. You had to smoke when you could nowadays. The flight had been less than two hours, smoke free. God, what a world it was getting to be. The next thing you knew there would be drink-free flights.

He all but bowled over the woman dressed like her grandmother.

"For baggage you go down that escalator."

She looked where he pointed, then back at him. Her eyes were unnerving. "Thank you."

"Lots of excitement back there," he said.

She walked beside him, a small thing, maybe five four. She was waiting for him to say more.

"They said she was the Moran girl. The Morans! The old man is dead but they're still after him. They couldn't nail him while he was alive." He leaned toward her. He felt safe saying such things to this little mouse. "A crook. Moran. One of the big ones."

It didn't get a rise out of her and he felt a sudden surge of anger at the thought that she was bothered by his cigarette. They had come to the escalator and he let her go first. From behind and above, her thick hair looked blue it was so black but here and there was a thread of silver. Maybe she was on parole from the funny farm. Could be. She sure seemed out of reach.

She stood some distance from the carousel while they waited for their bags to come tumbling down the chute. BGB, in the grips of his theory about the woman, looked around for

5

her keeper. He had been fooled by women before, don't get him started on that. His estimate sometimes was completely off. But this one really looked odd. Someone had to be meeting her. Alone she'd get lost for sure. It angered him that he felt half responsible for her, as if by talking to her he had given her claims on him. Standing there by herself, she seemed to be off in some world all her own.

A warning bell went off, the carousel lurched into motion and bags began to slide down the chute. With a tighter grip on the strap of his shoulder bag, the salesman pushed in close so he would be in position to grab the suitcase with the initials BGB on it. After half a dozen bags, he bet himself his would be last, maybe it would even be lost. He had the feeling it was going to be one of those days. That woman was a jinx. He glanced toward where she was standing.

She was no longer alone. Two other women were with her now. Women with veils. Nuns? And then it dawned on him who she was.

"Jesus Christ," he blurted out.

"Where?"

Another salesman nudged him in the ribs and laughed. After a moment, he laughed too. Ho ho. BGB always laughed when others did. It was like a religion. His suitcase had still not come when he watched the woman who had been on the plane with him walk off with the two nuns, one of whom had wrestled a strap-bound pigskin suitcase off the carousel.

No wonder he found her odd, BGB told himself. She was a nun, sure, but that was only the half of it.

That was Iggie Moran's daughter, he was sure of it. She was the passenger those reporters upstairs thought they had cornered, home from the convent to testify in her father's posthumous trial.

2

JOYCE WAS IN the backseat, Sister Mary Magdalene in the passenger seat and Kim at the wheel, her instructions to bring their guest swiftly but by an indirect route to the house on Walton Street. That Donna Moran had returned to Chicago and would be hiding out with them until she had to appear in court was to be kept secret.

"That poor nun," their passenger said. "She had no idea what was going on."

Joyce laughed. "That poor nun is an aspiring actress. Her name is Mildred Scott. How did she do?"

"Aspiring actress? She seemed middle-aged."

"A second career."

"What was her first?"

"What was Mary Magdalene's?"

"Joyce!"

"Well, it's true."

It seemed an inappropriate reminder, given Donna Moran's name in religion.

"A sinner?" their passenger said, and they all laughed. "I didn't notice her on the plane."

"She wasn't on it. She got onto the jetway under the pretense of meeting someone. She put the veil on and then emerged with the rest of you. It wouldn't have worked if you weren't wearing civvies."

Joyce seemed determined to say all the wrong things. Sister Mary Teresa's insistence to Sister Mary Magdalene's superior that she not arrive in Chicago in the habit of a discalced Carmelite had been eventually successful. When the Carmelite Mother Superior understood that Emtee Dempsey—as Sister Mary Teresa Dempsey was affectionately known in the house on Walton Street—still wore the traditional habit of the Order of Martha and Mary, she was mollified. No need to trouble with the sad decline of the M&M's. Once they had flourished; once Emtee Dempsey had taught history in the college the order ran west of the city. But in the madness that followed Vatican II, the sisters were gripped by the need for what was called relevance. Property was sold off, the college shut down, the nuns dispersed to swim in the sea of the people. In a very short time, there were but three left, Sister Mary Teresa and Sisters Kimberly and Joyce, withdrawn to this house on Walton Street, the gift of a grateful alumna. None of this was made known to the Carmelite Mother Superior. It was the prediction that Sister Mary Magdalene would be hounded by the press from the moment of her arrival that proved decisive.

"Is that why you're dressed as you are?" Sister Mary Magdalene asked.

Kim remained silent. Joyce could handle that question if she wanted to. Veils were not habit enough for the little Carmelite. The sense of being in the presence of someone come from another world had not diminished once they had gotten into the car. Although their guest was not wearing her religious habit, there was an unworldly air about her that set her off. In a pleasant, not a repellent way. Still, it set her off. One of the reasons Kim and Joyce and most other members of the M&M's—before the membership of the order had been reduced to the three of them in the house on Walton Street—

8

voted to dress in the fashion of the day was to remove the barrier of special dress and bring them closer to lay people. The main consequence was that they were ignored, passing unnoticed in the city. Dressed as a nun, Kim had always felt eyes on her, friendly and hostile eyes, curious and wary eyes, eyes that damned or canonized.

"We are meant to be a sign of contradiction," Emtee Dempsey said, glorying in the full skirt, cincture and clacking rosary, the wimple, and vast starched headdress that the Blessed Abigail Keineswegs had chosen as the distinctive dress of her daughters in religion. As for being a sign of contradiction, the old nun would have been that in a bathing suit.

Kim hoped they wouldn't be under the disapproving gaze of Sister Mary Magdalene while she was their guest on Walton Street.

"How does it look after all these years?" Joyce asked.

"What?"

"Chicago."

The Carmelite turned to look out the window beside her. Had she even noticed the city she had not seen in a dozen years?

"Now I know how Lazarus felt."

"Happy?"

Her laughter was throaty and unrestrained. "Of course you're right. Lazarus must have been delighted to be called back from the dead. But it isn't Our Lord who called me back. I'm here under obedience."

"And subpoena."

"I would have ignored that. We discussed it in chapter. Everyone agreed that in this case the law need not have been obeyed."

"But your superior ordered you to come?"

"She felt I owed it to my family."

Silence fell in the little Volkswagen bug, or as much silence as was compatible with the clatter of the motor and the general banging about because of the worn-out shock absorbers. That had been a new term for Emtee Dempsey when Joyce suggested they get new ones, offering to put them in herself. "Shock absorbers?" the old nun cried with delight. "I should have thought we *gave* shock riding about in that old car." And she was off on an etymological flight from which they returned only with difficulty to the topic of car repairs.

THREE

B AGS COMING DOWN the chute had jammed, and the carousel was turned off while the attendant got some boxes and suitcases and garment bags off by hand. There was no suitcase with BGB on it. By and large airline baggage systems worked but not always. That was why he would never have checked the shoulder bag. He looked around impatiently, to share his displeasure, and saw descending the escalator reporters from the contingent that had met his plane. He recognized the blond from Cable News.

"You got the wrong nun, didn't you?" BGB said, confronting her. She was about to ignore him, her eyes scanning the few passengers still at the baggage carousel, but then she gave him her full attention.

"Was there another?"

Up close and live, Linda Pastorini's face showed little lines of age, especially around the hard blue eyes. They darted now toward her colleagues. Make that rivals. She took BGB's arm and gestured with her head at her cameraman.

"Let's get away from here."

"I'm waiting for my suitcase."

For a minute he thought she was going to try to force him. She was certainly stronger than her cameraman, a boyish forty-year-old who wore his jeans low on his hips. The shirt under his open denim jacket was unbuttoned to the bottom of his rib cage.

"You saw her?"

"She walked right past all of you, came down here, took her bag and left."

Linda turned. "That door?"

"Yup."

"How was she dressed?"

"Like my Aunt Charlotte. Old. Dark clothes."

"Georgie, get the hell out there and see if she's still around."

Georgie made a wet impatient sound and flounced away.

The carousel started up again and BGB went back to wait for his bag. A last reporter was talking to a woman whose mouth turned down as she swung her head left and right. He left her in disgust. Linda Pastorini shrugged her shoulders as the other reporter went past. BGB had just spotted his suitcase when she said beside him, "Come on, I'll give you a lift."

"I'm going to the Stevenson."

"It's on my way."

It would have been nice to think she liked him, that he just happened to be a type she couldn't resist. Tough broad, at the end of a frustrating day, falls in with attractive salesman at the baggage carousel, a couple drinks, dinner, later on they would play house. In a world without mirrors he might have believed that. About the only thing he and Linda Pastorini had in common was that they both still smoked cigarettes.

"I can tell you everything I know right now. She came down just in front of me, stood right over there. Two nuns met her, and when her luggage came, off they went. Just like Georgie."

"Don't knock Georgie. He's a genius with a camera. You wouldn't have recognized the nuns?" She stopped, dragging

12

on her cigarette. "Listen to me, sounding like a reporter. So what if I missed her arrival? Everyone else did too."

He bowed to put his head through the strap of his shoulder bag, arranged it across his chest, and then picked up his suitcase.

"Need any help?"

She was just being nice. Or so he told himself, but for a mad moment his fantasies began again. He was growing on her. But when Georgie met them halfway to the door, she gestured, and he trained his camera on them.

"You say Donna Moran was on the plane with you?"

"What is this?"

She turned to the lens. "I'm speaking with one of the passengers on the flight from St. Louis on which Donna Moran, now Sister Mary Magdalene of the Carmelite Order, arrived in Chicago tonight." She turned to BGB. "When did you first realize the woman was Donna Moran?"

"She was standing next to me while all you reporters were bothering the other nun."

"She was ordinarily dressed?"

"I already told you."

A grim little smile. "Repeat it for our viewers." Trapped, he did. "You sound pretty knowledgeable about women's clothes."

"I'm in women's clothes." A practiced line, followed by a practiced laugh. "I represent F. X. Nicolo Creations of Milano and Chicago."

"What's your name?"

"Briggs, B. G. Briggs."

She flicked the switch on her microphone. "Thanks, B. G. It's not much, but it's more than the others got."

A belated sense of uneasiness swept over him. When would he learn to keep his goddam mouth shut?

But he had ceased to exist for Linda Pastorini. So much for the thought that his evening would be taken up by something more satisfying than a soft porn pay movie in his motel room.

13

"What was that all about?" It was a man who had come down the escalator with the reporters.

"What paper you with?"

"Hey. You think I'm a reporter?"

Knit tie, checkered shirt, rumpled London Fog topcoat. A far cry from Georgie. "Sorry."

"Why did she interview you?"

BGB pushed through into the chill Chicago evening air. He could catch a cab right here. He told the man what had brought Linda and the other reporters to O'Hare.

"You saw the Moran girl?"

"It had to be her. She was picked up by nuns. I can pick out a nun at two hundred yards. Had them in grade school. Plus these were wearing veils."

"Two others?"

BGB took up his station on the curb. "You sure you're not a reporter?"

The man laughed and punched him lightly on the arm. Just then a little Volkswagen bug went by.

"There they are," BGB cried. "That's her in the front seat."

FOUR

KATHERINE SENSKI HAD more lore on the Moran clan rattling around in her head than any other reporter in Chicago. But then she had half a century on most of them. Besides, she had followed the Moran saga throughout her career, not exclusively, of course, but when Ignatius Moran took over Moran Insurance from his father and began a forty-year reign, he soon was rumored to be involved in half the seamy things going on in the city. Iggie was what Katherine thought of as a professional Catholic, what would come to be called an ethnic Catholic, and that fascinated her. No one's perfect, but why should a crook go to church? He would have become wealthy on insurance alone, but then if he had been as honest as he always claimed, it was doubtful he would have sold so much insurance to the city.

It was the rare grand jury that did not have before it an investigation into something allegedly involving Iggie Moran; he was even indicted half a dozen times, but his only conviction, if it could be called that, had been for leaving the scene of an accident. His abandoned Chrysler was found driven halfway through a parked patrol car. Katherine uncovered the truth. The car had been driven by his son, Randy, a weak-chinned undergraduate at De Paul. She dug out the facts and wrote them up and earned the undying enmity of Iggie Moran. Earlier at a press club roast, Katherine had said that all Iggie Moran needed was a vowel movement to become an Iggie moron, but he had forgiven her that. She had never forgiven herself. However he lived his own life, Ignatius Moran was determined that his son and daughters should enjoy respectability. People could kid about him, within limits, but his family was out of bounds. After Katherine blew the whistle on his son, Iggie made the mistake of trying to get her fired. She was given a raise.

"They ever explain slander to you where you went to school?" Iggie asked when she confronted him in the lounge of the Palmer House, his favorite watering hole.

"I didn't want you found guilty of the one thing you're innocent of."

"Don't get funny with me." His smile never went away, as if the skull beneath the skin could not wait.

She had been no more successful than the prosecutor in linking him definitely to any of the things rumor linked him to. He gave half a million dollars to the Archdiocese of Chicago; the cardinal wavered but in the end accepted. How could he refuse without claiming to know more than he did? When Iggie died he was buried from the cathedral with great pomp and circumstance. The cortege tied up traffic in the Loop for two hours. That had been years ago. And then, posthumously, a young hotshot in the prosecutor's office managed to link Iggie Moran with the murder of Marilyn Derecho.

"Marilyn Derecho," Emtee Dempsey said. "May she rest in peace, poor girl. I gave her a C-."

Marilyn had been a classmate of Donna Moran at the college west of the city the Order of Martha and Mary had run until renewal had all but destroyed them. The college was sold and the proceeds given to the poor, that is, to members of the order who had taken the vow of poverty but now sought relevance in the inner city and elsewhere. Soon nuns were going over the wall like marines over an obstacle course. Donna and Marilyn had been in the last class to graduate from the college.

"She might have joined the Order of Martha and Mary in a better day," Emtee Dempsey said ambiguously, but Donna had been determined to become a Carmelite, like Thérèse of Lisieux. Iggie was equally determined that his daughter not become a nun. He was willing to be identified as a Catholic, but enough was enough. The fact that his daughter's best friend was as opposed to Donna's vocation as he was seemed to offer a way to dissuade Donna. He was otherwise very much taken by Marilyn Derecho. After Donna persisted and went off to the convent, it was said that Iggie more or less adopted Marilyn to take her place, an interpretation that did not flatter his other daughter, Lenore. But Lenore entertained no dreams of life as a nun, nor did she have any career ambitions. Like her mother, she was a background figure and like her mother apparently what she wanted was a husband and children and domestic routine. If Marilyn took Donna's place it was on a pedestal, untainted by his daily doings. He put her through Northwestern Law School, and she went to work for a Loop firm that would not have touched Iggie with a ten-foot pole. He was pleased as punch.

And devastated when she was found dead of a drug overdose. One of the rumors that swirled around Iggie was that he supplied the yuppies for whom cocaine was a symbol of chic. If this was true, and Katherine did not doubt it, and if Iggie ever permitted images of his clients to form in his mind, it was clear he had never dreamt that Marilyn Derecho could be among them. It was when Marilyn died that Iggie in his own way got religion too.

His wife, Florence, a long-suffering beauty from County Mayo, was a daily communicant, and lo and behold suddenly there was Iggie himself by her side at early morning Mass at St. Peter's. Katherine checked out the rumor herself and felt like a Pharisee for resenting Iggie's apparent conversion. He began to give away money with abandon. If heaven could be bought, Iggie was willing to pay the price.

He bequeathed the archdiocese another half million dollars, a fateful gift. It was the accusation by a group of disgruntled Catholics that the cardinal had knowingly accepted ill-gotten gains that occasioned Randy Moran's libel suit against the Archdiocese of Chicago. The cardinal, attempting a Solomonic solution, promised to divert the Moran money, plus the interest it would have accrued, to providing shelter for the homeless. This apparent acceptance of the charge that money from Ignatius Moran was tainted was more than Randy, or his lawyers, could bear. The archdiocese offered to name the shelter after Ignatius Moran. Randy's lawyers slapped another suit on the archdiocese for diversion and misuse of funds, unauthorized use of the deceased's name and other arcane misdemeanors. In defense of the cardinal's agreement that Ignatius Moran was not an ideal donor, the archdiocesan lawyers pointed to the prosecutor's contention that Moran had been amorously involved with Marilyn Derecho and was criminally responsible for her death. Meanwhile, Wiley, the prosecutor, subpoenaed Sister Mary Magdalene, née Donna Moran, for appearance before the grand jury. If all these legal and litigious moves and countermoves led to the courtroom, it would be Iggie Moran on posthumous trial for the murder of Marilyn Derecho.

"I half expect young Moran to bring a personal suit against the cardinal," Emtee Dempsey keened, rocking back and forth in agony that such things had come to be.

"Good Lord," Katherine said. "Don't say that out loud."

"I hope my giving refuge to Sister Mary Magdalene will not be construed as taking sides."

"I hope it will remain a secret."

●

Now, on the night of Donna Moran's return to Chicago, Katherine got out of a taxi in front of the house on Walton

Street and looked up the street to see if the little Volkswagen was parked there. It was. And there was a man looking it over suspiciously.

"Does that car interest you?" Katherine asked.

The man leapt in surprise, but then she had come up behind him noiselessly.

"Is it yours?"

"Why do you ask?"

She could not place him, but he was vaguely familiar. He looked sheepish. Hands plunged into the pockets of his rumpled London Fog topcoat, he tried to smile. "I'm more interested in that house."

He pointed at the house, designed by Frank Lloyd Wright, the gift of an alumna, one of the fragments of M&M property Sister Mary Teresa had rescued from the ruin of the order and where she lived with Sisters Kimberly and Joyce. On this night of all nights, curiosity about that house seemed a threat.

"Who are you?"

Again the unsuccessful smile. Then he shrugged, as if giving up. He couldn't fool her. "I'm a reporter."

"Really?" A publisher perhaps, but not a reporter. "What paper?"

"The *Tribune*."

"No, you're not."

"Why do you doubt me?"

"Because I've been employed by the *Tribune* longer than any other living human being and I have never seen you before in my life."

"All right, I lied. That's an extraordinary house."

"This is an extraordinary time of day to be admiring it. And this car."

He agreed with her. He thanked her. He turned and walked rapidly up the street, his open topcoat flapping in the breeze coming in off the lake. Katherine was filled with foreboding as she mounted the steps to the door.

5

WHEN THE CARMELITE nun entered Emtee Dempsey's study she came alive for the first time, or so Kim thought watching her. Their guest stopped inside the door of the study to look at the little old nun seated behind the desk, and her face lit up. Emtee Dempsey rose and the young nun ran into her arms.

"Sister Mary Teresa, it is so good to see you again!"

Tears glistened in Emtee Dempsey's eyes. Like many sentimental people she was loath to show her emotions, but she lived for reunions with her old students, and Sister Mary Magdalene was a very special case.

"Will you drink cocoa?" she demanded when she had blinked her eyes dry.

"I'd love some cocoa."

"Sister Joyce!" Emtee Dempsey cried.

"I'll tell her," Kim offered. "You two have so much to talk about."

In the kitchen, Joyce whispered, "She makes me feel like an imposter."

"She's cloistered, we're not."

"That's what I mean."

Kim was spared the task of interpreting that by the arrival of Katherine Senski. With her usual panache, Katherine was wearing a cape, a velvet beret festooned with sequins and a brooch that seemed a badge of office.

"Is she here?"

"Everything went off perfectly."

Katherine dipped her head and looked with her pouched eyes at Kim. "Not quite, my dear. I think you were followed."

Kim protested, trying to tell Katherine how well Mildred Scott had done her job, but the old reporter made a dismissive gesture with her hand.

"There was a man outside examining your car. When I confronted him, he brashly asked who lived in this house."

"But people are always asking about this house. As for the car, well, they don't make them like that anymore. We've had offers."

Katherine inhaled through her nose, deeply, meaning she did not intend to argue the point. "In the study?"

"Yes. Do you want cocoa?"

"I am a woman of the world, not a nun. I want bourbon."

Sister Mary Magdalene was anything but a woman of the world. But during the next hour, as she answered questions about her convent and then followed the bantering repartee between Katherine and Emtee Dempsey, she came out of her shell. She was, Kim realized, a very beautiful woman, despite her clothing and the severe way she wore her hair. But it was soon apparent that she was a very tired young lady too. She had been up since five o'clock that morning, had been driven to the St. Louis airport after observing the community schedule until noon and now, despite the joy in being in the presence of her old teacher, she was, under the soporific influence of Joyce's cocoa, soon nodding in her chair.

"Off to bed with you," Emtee Dempsey commanded. "We

can talk in the morning. Sister Kimberly, show Sister her room."

Sister Mary Magdalene would be next to Emtee Dempsey in the second-floor wing, where they all had their rooms. They stopped in the chapel for a visit before going upstairs.

"We no longer have a chaplain, so we go to the cathedral in the morning. Mass is at seven."

"Seven."

Kim realized that Sister Magdalene was surprised at the lateness, not the earliness, of the hour. How cruel it was that Sister Mary Magdalene had been summoned from her cloister to become embroiled in the lawsuits raging over her late father.

"And involving her best friend," Emtee Dempsey said, shaking her head. "Poor Marilyn, God rest her soul. Katherine, are these insinuations true?"

"About Iggie and Marilyn? I'm afraid so."

Wiley, the prosecutor who had pursued the spoor of Iggie Moran long after the object of his zeal had gone to that bourne from which no traveler returns, was said to have eyewitness testimony and physical evidence that no one other than Iggie Moran could have killed Marilyn. Katherine was surprised by this, since the manager and other residents of the building in which Marilyn had her apartment and where her body was found had claimed not even to know the name of Iggie Moran, let alone to have seen him on the premises. Perhaps Wiley had the testimony of headwaiters and bartenders no longer silent because of fear of reprisals. But what physical evidence could there be now, years later?

Katherine did not at all doubt the basic premise. That Iggie and Marilyn had been lovers was inescapable.

"Why?" In matters of the heart, Emtee Dempsey deferred to Katherine who, though she had never married, had lived her life under the romantic cloud of a doomed love, and this conferred expert status on her in the house on Walton Street.

"The cynic would say she was using him," Katherine said, after a moment's judicious pause. "The chauvinist would insist he was using her."

"What would you say?"

"That they were in love. I despised Iggie Moran. He treated his own children despicably. His wife was a saint or a masochist or both. He spent his life exploiting others. There had always been another woman in his life, a floozy, someone to be used and discarded. Marilyn was different."

"That, if you are right, accounts for him. But Marilyn?"

Katherine looked over both shoulders and then at Kim and Emtee Dempsey. "I would only say this here and to you two. There is something in a woman's heart that seeks humiliation, that wants to be trampled on. And there is the fascination of evil. A combination of these drew Marilyn to Iggie Moran."

"Original Sin," the old nun murmured.

"I only wish it were."

"Katherine, did you tell Sister of the man outside?" Kim asked.

"Just a curious passerby," Emtee Dempsey said dismissively. "We have them all the time."

Kim didn't know if Katherine was deceived, but it was clear to her that Emtee Dempsey was not indifferent to the news that a stranger had been prowling about their car.

"I felt I should know him," Katherine said.

"Would you like more whiskey, Katherine?"

"Good heavens, no. I must get home. Who is to be told that Sister Mary Magdalene has arrived in Chicago?"

"Told? No one."

Katherine, on her feet, looked sternly at her old friend. "Sister Mary Teresa, you did not bring that woman to Chicago with the intention of keeping it a secret from everyone."

"Mr. Rush will come in the morning and advise us on how best to proceed. The purpose of Sister's visit is to vindicate her father's memory. And Marilyn Derecho's. After what you

23

have told me, she might as well have remained in Missouri and ignored the subpoena."

Katherine stood frowning over this uncharacteristically self-critical statement. Abruptly she sat down again and announced she would have another drink.

"Just a half glass," she insisted, but added, "no ice."

six

A T SEVENTY-FIVE BENJAMIN Rush considered himself in the penultimate stage of his legal career. He continued to attract business to the firm, but actual work was left to the junior partners while his own time was devoted to the affairs of clients of long standing, a dwindling list to whom his sense of loyalty grew as their numbers decreased, but his client of preference was Sister Mary Teresa Dempsey and what was left of the Order of Martha and Mary.

That an order once so thriving and influential in the educational and religious life of the city should have all but disappeared before one's very eyes had become a metaphor of life to him. He drew no mordant satisfaction from the conviction that all things pass away, but it was a truth that age and experience made inescapable. To recognize such truths and yet retain composure, even optimism, was a special grace. It was not one he claimed for himself, but it was what he especially admired in the old nun, whose students had called her Emtee Dempsey. The Book of Job had become a favorite of Benjamin Rush and he relished that poor patriarch's rejection of the accusation that everything had been taken from him as a punishment for his sins. Job wrangled with his friends and complained to God. It was an attitude one could understand, but it was, after all, based on the assumption that we are the best judges of what happens to us. There was not a trace of Job in Emtee Dempsey. Well, perhaps a trace. The Lord gives and the Lord takes away might have been her motto.

"Why should you suffer so?" Katherine Senski had asked in anguish in the dark days when Sister Mary Teresa had been attacked for intransigence by her sisters in religion.

"Why should I have been blessed is a better question, Katherine. And who are we to say that all this is so bad?"

Not that his old friend had seen the shutting down of the college and the selling of the property as anything but a grievous mistake. She had argued long and well against this move, and she had lost. That the victors were all too soon out of the order did not undo the damage they had done. Rush had helped Emtee Dempsey with her fallback position, retaining the house on Walton Street and the property in Indiana on the lake shore. When the tumult and shouting were over, when the order had been reduced to the three women on Walton Street and Emtee Dempsey settled down to the chore of writing a comprehensive history of the twelfth century, Benjamin Rush learned to rejoice at the outcome. The old nun kept urging him to read a novel by H. F. Prescott called *The Man on a Donkey*. She assured him it would prove to him that her plight was not new in the history of the Church. From time to time, he was called into service on Sister Mary Teresa's behalf, and he was more than happy to be of help. More often than not, his advice was ignored, but this did not cause him to waver in his loyalty. The Donna Moran incident was the latest decision Emtee Dempsey had made against his best advice.

"Tell the woman to stay there in her convent. Nothing but trouble can come from returning to Chicago to become involved in these Byzantine quarrels. The archdiocese should never have accepted that money, but if they had simply returned it to Randolph Moran, I am sure that would have been the end of it."

"It's too bad you didn't advise them, Bejamin."

"But that is the advice they were given."

The old nun shook her head incredulously, as if the thought of a client refusing his lawyer's advice was beyond her comprehension.

"But they served a subpoena on the Moran girl in her convent in Missouri."

"No one is going to remove her bodily from a cloistered convent."

"You don't think the good name of Ignatius Moran is worth defending?"

"He had none."

"But the young woman, my former student . . ."

Rush had noticed in Emtee Dempsey a certain reluctance to accept concrete instances of the depths of folly into which sex can plunge the otherwise sane. True, she professed to believe that ninety-five percent of the world's woe was because of sexual misbehavior. She cited Pascal to the effect that the history of the world might have been different had Cleopatra's nose been a trifle longer. She had a firm theoretical grasp of the point, but it was a learned, not an experienced, truth.

"Sister, there seems little doubt that Marilyn Derecho was Ignatius Moran's mistress."

The old nun winced. She said nothing, but he could tell by the set of her head that she had not accepted it. It seemed inescapable that she meant to encourage the Moran girl to leave her cloistered convent in another state and come back to Chicago to defend the name of her roguish father and the reputation of a friend who had become his kept woman.

Nor was she deterred by Randy Moran's opposition. Rush had been summoned to Walton Street on the day Sister Mary Teresa agreed to see the son and heir of Iggie Moran. Physiognomy is not character, as Emtee Dempsey later put it, but Randy Moran was not well served by his receding chin and hooded eyes. Iggie had been physically impressive, even handsome in a glittering way, but his son was a throwback to the bogs of the old country, someone meant to scratch a mere subsistence from unfriendly soil. He was a rich man, but wealth conferred neither confidence nor authority on him. And he made the enormous mistake of issuing orders to Sister Mary Teresa.

"You talk Donna into coming to Chicago and I'll do to you what I'm doing to the cardinal."

"You put me in eminent company," the old nun purred.

"I mean it. I could have this property condemned."

"It was designed by Frank Lloyd Wright, Mr. Moran," Rush intervened. "It is a national monument."

"Yeah?"

That Randolph Moran should have cast himself in the role of one indignant that the Archdiocese of Chicago would not take a million dollars, a significant portion of which might have been his own, was on the face of it improbable. Sister Mary Teresa told him this, and something like a leer took possession of his narrow face.

"The best of both worlds, Sister. I'll end up with the money and probably damages as well. Nobody treats my family like that and gets away with it."

Rush said, "Is it your family that has brought these suits or yourself alone?"

"I'm acting for the family! And that includes Donna. Because she's a nun they think she's on their side, but they're wrong." He turned to the old nun. "So keep out of this."

"Who told you I was in it?"

He looked sly. "Never mind."

"In any case, I'm sure your sister will do whatever she thinks is right."

For a moment Randy looked as if he would take umbrage at that, but he decided he had already said what he came to say. He banged his way down the hall, and the front door slammed after him.

"You know I would never suggest that a religious vocation is an escape, Bejamin, but aren't the ways of God marvelous? Donna Moran is providentially called to a religious life, which removes her from the city in which that young man lives."

That had been two months ago. On this October morning Rush arrived at Walton Street to meet with Sister Mary Teresa and the guest he assumed had arrived safely the night before, but when he turned the corner onto Walton there seemed to be a small riot going on in front of the house. Traffic was backed up because cars and TV station vans were double-parked on both sides of the street while several police cruisers, their rooftop lights revolving in angry yellow flashes, seemed to add to the confusion. But if the street was crowded, the sidewalk in front of the house was jammed. People milled about on the walk, some stood on the porch steps, their further passage barred by two men in civilian clothes but unmistakably policemen. Rush recognized them as Gleason and O'Connell, the minions of Lieutenant Richard Moriarity.

Benjamin Rush braked his car and began cautiously to back into the street from which he had come. This maneuver was accompanied by an orchestral burst of angry horns, but the distinguished lawyer ignored these comments. A space at curbside opened up after he had threaded his way in reverse for a third of the block, a space that seemed to be waiting just for him. More accurately for fire department equipment, as the fireplug at the curb suggested, but this was an emergency that excused the way he had backed down the street and could easily cover claiming this provident parking space as well. Benjamin Rush was no scofflaw, he could be eloquent on the theme that ours is a government of laws and not of men, but when all is said and done, law is our servant, not our master. Besides, he was consumed with curiosity to learn what had drawn all these people to the house on Walton Street.

SEVEN 7

YOU NEVER KNEW which story would fly.

Linda Pastorini, cupping her cigarette and turning away from the street, as if she could smoke and not smoke at the same time, glanced at the house. Frank Lloyd Wright, the prairie style. But a house is a setting as well as a building, and Walton Street had not been kind to its claimant for architectural fame. The house was now bracketed by undistinguished apartment buildings five stories high, a height sufficient to rob the house's roofline and distinctive eaves of their power to control space. Linda's first husband had been an architect, and such lore clung to her mind along with other reminders of what a mistake that marriage had been. So had her second. Single again, free at last, she was at thirty-seven beginning to make her name on cable television.

Which meant she had had some lucky breaks. This story was one of them. The anonymous call telling her that Donna Moran would be slipping into the city last night had obviously not been an exclusive. Reporters had been tripping over one another in the waiting area, the print media, every local station, all of them resentful of the others, since each had come with the idea that this was a scoop. What a herd. It still rankled Linda that she had taken the bait with the rest of them and allowed Donna Moran to walk right past them all.

BGB. She smiled. Short, overweight, self-indulgent smile, kind of like Willie, her second husband. Particularly when he teased her about going for the wrong nun. The little interview with him had been done half out of spite, half to persuade Georgie this wasn't a wild goose chase.

"Wild goose? Don't you dare." Georgie was older than she was, but he reminded Linda of playgrounds, kid stuff.

They ran the interview with Briggs on the hour from ten o'clock. Other channels picked it up, the morning paper was full of it. Moran Daughter in Chicago. Linda woke up to her ringing phone. The station. Zeke Toggle was ecstatic.

"You've done it again, girl. We're the only ones who had it."

By then there was more. On a morning talk show, Mildred Scott, an actress, claimed that she had been hired to impersonate a nun and distract the press corps while a real nun got off the plane from St. Louis. The actress smirked at the camera, eliciting memories of Alan Funt at his worst. But it turned out she had no idea who the real nun was.

"But real nuns hired me!" she cried, to regain ground.

"What real nuns?"

That was when Mildred mentioned Sister Mary Teresa Dempsey and this house on Walton Street, which was why Linda and Georgie and God knows how many other journalists were now milling about in the forlorn hope that there would be something to report. Georgie was scooting around, getting lots of footage, making a bit of a display of himself. Linda watched him back into Rollo Lobund, the hotshot from WBBM, then excuse himself profusely. Artist at work. Lobund turned away disdainfully. Ah well, Georgie was used to rebuffs. Working with Georgie could make becoming a nun seem almost attractive.

"You're the slave of your loins, Georgie," she told him.

He busied himself to see how many other words he could derive from the letters spelling *loins*. Did he have a reflective bone in his body?

"Careful," he warned. "Lions. Oil. Soil. Silo . . ."

She tuned him out. At least they were on this assignment that, however boring, was where the media action of the moment was. What could compete with a kidnapped Carmelite, following on the hoopla at O'Hare the night before?

The house did not look like a convent. Imagine living right here in the middle of the city. But what was the point of it? Linda had called in to the station and listened to what Zeke had dug up on the Order of Martha and Mary. Back a few years, before Linda had come to Chicago, the order had been something, running its own college. There were still lots of alumnae whose loyalty to their school was undimmed by its closing. "Like being faithful to a former husband," Linda suggested, but all she got from Zeke was a moment of silence. What Zeke gave her was enough for a remote, for which she muscled her way up the porch steps while Georgie positioned himself in such a way that the house would be the background. Several reporters took notes on what she said. She repeated what Zeke told her, and they would repeat what she said. Was this really the life she wanted?

Les Allegro, the morning anchor, had questions for her and she bantered with him for several minutes, conveying what it was like out here on Walton Street in front of the house to which, presumably, Donna Moran, now Sister Mary Magdalene of the Carmelite Order, had been taken last night. The investigations into the activities of Ignatius Moran had gone on, years after his death, crescendoing, as Allegro put it, with the recent charges that Moran senior had been responsible for the death of his young companion, Marilyn Derecho. After several minutes trading information that had been fed them by Zeke, they closed down.

"Why are they called Carmelites?" she asked Georgie, who claimed to be Catholic.

He thought about it. "Because they give up candy?"

That's when she lit up the cigarette. It was nearly ten o'clock. She'd begun the day with the thought that she no longer smoked, she used to, not anymore, but then she began every day that way. Ten o'clock was early to give in, but she inhaled deeply, needing it. The untold secret about journalism is that it is boring.

"If we were alone, I could open that door," Georgie said, and Linda smiled. Among Georgie's talents were some that would have made him a successful thief. Linda found this out when she lost her door key and Georgie, incredibly, let her in with a credit card. "How did you do that?" she'd asked. He showed her. She learned how to do it. On boring days, he acquainted her with different ways of opening different kinds of doors.

"Handy," she said.

"You never know."

She was pushed aside when one of the cops guarding the steps made way for a distinguished-looking elderly man in a black cashmere coat and homburg. Mr. Rush. Who the hell is Mr. Rush?

"A lawyer," the *Sun-Times* said.

"Whose?"

"Good question. Mr. Rush, are you representing Donna Moran?"

With what she would later describe as a patrician air, Mr. Rush glanced at the reporter who threw this question at him.

"No."

RUSH DENIES MORAN CLIENT. That was the enigmatic headline that would suggest to the unwary reader that a passing denial had been a formal repudiation.

"I think I want to be a nun," she said to Georgie.
"It takes more than dressing up."
"You remember that."
He giggled and punched her arm.

EIGHT

KATHERINE WAS THERE, Richard was there, a Mr. Butler representing the cardinal was there, and now Mr. Rush arrived.

"Benjamin, thank God you've come. I made the mistake of admitting these people to the house and now I seem unable to get rid of them."

Kim marveled at the old nun's composure. No wonder Richard did not believe her ringing assertion that Sister Mary Magdalene Moran was not in this house. But it was true. Kim herself was still stunned by the events of the morning.

She was used to finding Sister Mary Teresa already in the chapel when she came downstairs, but this morning their Carmelite guest was also there and, like Emtee Dempsey, deep in meditation. It was 6:00 A.M. Houses of religion had for centuries ordered their days according to the liturgical hours, which bear a loose relation to the sun's daily trip from east to west. Monks had gone to bed when the sun went down but were up at two in the morning to chant the early hours, settling down again afterward until dawn broke and a day began in which work and prayer alternated. A day in the Order of

Martha and Mary had never been so austere, although Blessed Abigail assumed they would be up before dawn for Mass and meditation. Their schedule was less rigorous now than it had been, a not infrequent observation of Emtee Dempsey, who loved to regale Joyce and Kim with stories of how demanding things had been when she first entered the order. She had not fought all the changes introduced in recent years, saving her fire for the most important issues. But she herself hewed as closely as she ever had to the rule in its original interpretation. As a Carmelite, Sister Mary Magdalene, of course, was used to an ascetic life and a day that began very early.

"Better stay here," Emtee Dempsey said to their guest when they were preparing to set out for the cathedral and mass.

"But I must go to Mass."

Tiny eyes brightened behind rimless glasses. Emtee Dempsey was for the nonce Sister Mary Magdalene's religious superior and, although she was not loath to invoke obedience, she preferred to do this indirectly.

"No."

A mircrosecond went by and then the young nun bowed her head. "What shall I do while you're gone?"

"You can remain in chapel."

"Should I put on coffee?"

Emtee Dempsey looked at Joyce. The kitchen was Joyce's domain.

"It's all set, Sister," Joyce said. "I just flick it on when we get back."

So they left the young Carmelite in the chapel and set out for Holy Name Cathedral, as they did each morning, though on this occasion Emtee Dempsey vowed that she would seek at least a temporary chaplain so that they could have morning Mass in their own chapel.

Sister Mary Magdalene was not in the chapel when they returned an hour later. Nor was she in her room. A quick and increasingly panicky search made it clear that she was nowhere in the house. The three nuns stood in the kitchen, staring at one another. Sister Mary Teresa's face was pale with the implications of the inescapable fact.

The young Carmelite who had come under the safety of their roof was gone!

"Maybe she decided to go to Mass anyway," Joyce said.

Emtee Dempsey considered it. "I don't think so."

"The door was locked when we returned."

Joyce said, "It locks itself."

"She turned on the coffee," Kim said.

And for a moment the three of them stood inhaling the aroma of coffee, as if it were a denial of the fact that Sister Mary Magdalene was gone.

"She is not in the house," Emtee Dempsey said, the words costing her an effort. Perhaps she was remembering the solemn assurances she had given the young Carmelite's superior in Missouri. "Either she left the house voluntarily or she did not. To leave voluntarily would have violated obedience. That means she left involuntarily."

"Force? But no one could get inside."

"The wicked have ruses," the old nun said. "Put not your trust in dead bolt locks."

But it was difficult to imagine what Emtee Dempsey was suggesting. Sister Mary Magdalene would have had to open either the front door or the back, that led off the kitchen. A swift inspection of the back door ruled out that exit. Joyce had leaned her ironing board against it, and the ironing board was still in place. The front door then. If someone had rung the bell or knocked, it was possible to see who it was from either of two vantage points. The door itself, which had a peephole, or from the closet, where another peephole, afforded a side view of anyone at the door. But Sister Mary Magdalene would not have known that. They had not thought to instruct her on what to do if someone came calling. After all, they would be back before eight.

"Someone came and she opened the door to them. Why? You will say that years in a cloister made her naive. Quite the contrary. Her training would work against her opening the convent door to anyone. Yet she did. That means she knew the caller."

"Sister, all this is just make-believe."

Emtee Dempsey tilted her head and looked at Kim. "I think of it as logic."

Joyce said, "I say she just went for a walk. How long has it been since she's seen Chicago? She looked out, saw what a fine day it is, and stepped outside. I'll bet she got lost!"

Joyce was immediately in the grips of her own theory and insisted on canvasing the neighborhood in search of the missing Carmelite. When she had left, Kim said, "I'll call Richard if you'd like." She said it in the expectation that the old nun would react angrily to the suggestion.

"Good idea. A kidnapping should be reported at once."

A kidnapping! Kim bit her tongue and went to the phone. Richard was not at home and he had not yet arrived at police headquarters. Kim was almost relieved. She had dreaded talking to her brother with Emtee Dempsey in the room, given the withering skepticism with which she was sure he would greet her call. A minute after she hung up, the front doorbell rang. Kim ran to answer it. When she looked through the peephole, she expelled breath in angry disappointment. Her brother, Lieutenant Richard Moriarity, stood on the porch, glaring at the peephole with fire in his eye. Kim opened the door to him with mixed emotions. He pushed past her and was about to start down the hall toward the study when Emtee Dempsey appeared in the doorway of the kitchen.

"Richard! We were just trying to reach you. Your lovely wife said you were on your way to your office. Thank God you came by here."

"Where is Donna Moran?" His manner suggested that he was prepared to disbelieve any answer she gave him. The old nun's face filled with sorrow.

"Then you have no news of her?"

Kim had often warned Richard about using profanity in this

house, but in moments of stress he was likely to forget, and most moments in this house were stressful for him.

"Damn it, I know she's here. It's in the paper, it's on television. I know all about the stunt you pulled at O'Hare. Mildred Scott has sung like a bird, so let's cut out the crap. Where is she?"

"Richard!" Kim cried. "Stop. You don't understand. She *was* here. She spent the night in this house. But when we came back from Mass she was gone."

"Don't Carmelites go to Mass?"

Emtee Dempsey, the soul of patience, took Richard's arm and led him to the table. "Get Richard some coffee, Sister. He has every right to react as he has." She sat across from him and spoke solemnly. "Sister Mary Magdalene has been the victim of foul play, Richard. I'm sure of it."

Kim kept out of range of Richard's eyes while Emtee Dempsey developed for him her train of thought. He found it more logical than Kim did, thank God. He liked the suggestion that Sister Mary Magdalene had opened the door because she knew the caller.

"Randy Moran," he said, slamming a hand on the table. Kim put a mug of coffee next to the hand and withdrew.

"Oh, I don't think so, Richard. There had been a falling out among the three Morans, Randolph, Lenore, Sister Mary Magdalene."

"A nun holding a grudge?" Richard said, affecting disbelief.

Emtee Dempsey smiled sweetly. "I was thinking of her brother."

Richard sipped the coffee then demanded to be shown where Sister Mary Magdalene had spent the night. Emtee Dempsey nodded and Kim led her brother upstairs.

"Kim, how does she manage to get involved in things like this? You keep telling me she's smart. Someday I'd like to have a smidgen of evidence that she is. The Moran trial is going to make mincemeat of anyone who goes near it. It's a no-win situation. And don't tell me she's worried about the cardinal."

"We offered a cloistered nun asylum during her visit to Chicago," Kim said patiently. "If that is being involved, well, then we are."

"Asylum! Then where is she?"

He stood in the hallway, looking into the room where their guest had spent the night, although there was scant evidence of it. The bed was made, everything was spick-and-span, but the pigskin suitcase on the floor was proof enough of occupancy. Richard lifted the cover. The suitcase contained a habit, clearly not that of the Order of Martha and Mary.

As they came downstairs, the sound of voices lifted to them. The front door was open. The man on the porch was a stranger to Kim, but Richard recognized him. He opened the door wide.

"What is it, Butler?"

"I'm here to speak with Sister Mary Magdalene Moran. On behalf of the cardinal."

Richard looked beyond Butler where the first television van was pulling into the curb. He took Butler's arm, pulled him inside and closed the door firmly. He turned to Joyce.

"Don't answer any more rings."

"Good idea," Sister Mary Teresa said, emerging from the kitchen. She peered up at Butler.

"Philip Butler, Sister. With Swift, Swallow, Finch, and Robinson. We're representing the archdiocese. I've come to see Sister Mary Magdalene."

"Were you here last night?"

Butler cocked his head and frowned. "Last night I had hoped to see Sister Mary Magdalene at the airport. Like many others, I was disappointed."

"You missed her at the airport?" She started down the hall with young Butler, and Kim and Richard fell in behind. "How did you know she was coming in?"

"We got a call."

"From whom?"

"She didn't say."

"Quite a number of people got similar calls," Emtee Dempsey said, settling behind her desk and indicating to Philip Butler that he should sit across from her. "I'm told the press was there in force."

"Mildred," Joyce said, a faint disgust in her voice. "I should have known she'd try to use this."

"Mildred Scott has been a busy bee," Richard said. "She's in the papers, on TV." He shook his head. "It serves you right. You tried to con everyone else, and she conned you."

Philip Butler followed this exchange with a confused expression. "When can I see Sister Mary Magdalene?" he asked, seemingly unsure to whom the question ought to be addressed.

"Sister is not in the house," Emtee Dempsey told him.

Butler looked concerned. "If Moran's lawyers get hold of her first . . ." He looked around almost wildly, as if this were a prospect too terrible to contemplate. "Where is she?"

●

Two hours later, they still did not have the answer to that question. Outside, the mob of media people increased, a traffic jam formed, Mr. Rush arrived and, after consulting with Emtee Dempsey, took Butler into the living room under instructions to find out just what Swift, Swallow, Finch, and Robinson expected of Sister Mary Magdalene that would be beneficial for their client, the cardinal archbishop of Chicago. Katherine had been brought into the house behind the flying wedge formed by Gleason and O'Connell. She found it hard not to wear an expression of satisfaction as she sailed through her protesting colleagues to the house. But her expression turned grim once the door was shut behind her. She looked meaningfully at Kim.

"The study?"

"Yes."

41

Katherine marched down the hall, her arms swinging in wide arcs. Inside the study, she stopped.

"Someone telephoned me. I came directly here to tell you. I wrote it down."

Katherine opened her purse and took out a folded piece of paper. She brought it within range of her bifocal inserts, paused, then read.

"Sister Mary Magdalene is no more."

"What!"

Katherine handed the paper to Emtee Dempsey. Kim got behind her and read it over her shoulder.

Sister Mary Magdalene is no more.

TWO

1

W HEN HE REPLACED the phone after taking his wake-up call, Briggs groped for the remote control and flicked on the TV. The familiar faces on the morning show made him feel as much at home as he ever did. He stumbled into the bathroom and a moment later, under the pelting shower, felt the effects of last night's drinking wash away. It was when he was shaving, the mirror tilted so he could see the television in the room, that he saw himself twice.

He went into the room and stood openmouthed, watching and listening to himself being interviewed by the broad from Cable News. Linda Pastorini. She turned and looked at the camera, identifying herself. And then the local anchor took over, talking of the disappearance of Donna Moran.

Briggs, half his face still frothing with shaving cream, sat on the end of the bed and stared at the television screen. What was he waiting for? That was it. It was over. He tried the other local channels, but there was nothing further on the missing nun. A report on the gangland murder of an alleged drug dealer momentarily caught his attention. Back in the bathroom, scraping the half-dried lather from his face, he was filled with fear. It was stupid to be publicly linked with anything involving the late Iggie Moran. It wasn't good for business. It was dangerous.

When his breakfast arrived it made him jumpy. He didn't remember hanging the order on his door last night. But he must have. He had to watch the drinking. More than one good man had been undone by it. It was an occupational hazard of a life spent on the road. The waiter put the tray on the desk and Briggs signed for it. From the looks of the tray, he'd gone to bed with an appetite, ordering all that. He ate swiftly, bacon, eggs, biscuits with lots of butter and jam, just what the doctor didn't order. There were barely two cups in the coffee pot. He was on the second when the local news came on again.

The Linda Pastorini interview was on and off the screen in seconds, but his face seemed to linger there. What a goddam fool he was, blathering like that. Granted he'd been tricked into it, but he could have refused to cooperate. They couldn't have run the film if he had told Linda Pastorini to go to hell. She showed up on a live report from the house from which the nun was missing. Brassy bitch. But there was something attractive about her, the attraction of a woman who seemed to have the same attitude toward a little fun as a man did. He remembered his raunchy hopes at the terminal, but what he felt for her now was anger rather than lust. How many people would see him shooting off his mouth about the daughter of Iggie Moran? But there was only one he was really worried about.

Then he remembered the guy who had come up to him at the taxi stand, the one he'd thought was another reporter, and what stuck in his memory was the way he had pointed out to the guy the Moran daughter as she was being driven away by the two nuns. Briggs sat, holding his coffee in both hands, his eyes out of focus. Had he fingered the daughter for whoever had snatched her? The guy in the topcoat ran off as soon as Briggs pointed to the VW. Had he followed the nuns to their house?

Whatever he had felt before was nothing to what he felt

now. If he had been the link between the nun and her kidnappers, he was in deep trouble. He could identify the man to whom he'd pointed out the Moran daughter. If that was her kidnapper. . . . Irrationally, he blamed it all on Linda Pastorini.

The house on Walton Street was not half a mile from his hotel. Briggs took just his shoulder bag and went out into the chill sunlit Chicago morning. He was free until ten o'clock; he had time. He might have been out for a stroll to work off the effects of last night and of his cholesterol-chocked breakfast, but there was an exercise gym in the hotel if that had been his intention. Who was he trying to kid? Himself, that's who. It was a damned fool thing to get any more involved in the Moran business than he already was, but he wouldn't mind a chance to tell Linda Pastorini what he thought of her. Professionally, that is.

He smiled. Last night's fantasies were suddenly stronger than this morning's fear and anger. The streets were full of harried females on their way to work, all dolled up but wearing sneakers, their heels in plastic bags or stashed at the office. Whether they worked or not, women couldn't resist dressing to attract, to arouse. It was their nature. And it was the male's nature to respond. The workplace had changed over the last decade. Briggs was dealing with more women than ever before, and not just the secretaries. Affirmative action was moving them into positions of some power. Briggs wouldn't have minded a little affirmative action of his own.

The busy noisy street, all these people going in a dozen directions, hurry, hurry, made him feel less lonely. He felt part of this, an anonymous part, but a part nonetheless. Some of these people must have seen him on television. He half feared, half hoped to surprise a look of recognition from passersby. Is this what it was like to be a celebrity? From time to time, in an airport, he spotted a sports star or television personality, convoyed by three or four others, their eyes sweeping the area, avoiding eye contact, expecting to be recognized. Briggs had always thought less of them for that hunger to be known by strangers. But it must be exhilarating. He himself could not even catch a passing eye.

When he got to Walton Street he could see the jam of media trucks a block away. He should have turned then and gone back to his hotel. He had no business nosing into a Chicago kidnapping. The connection with the Morans made it dangerous. It was one of those moments when doing or not doing something really mattered. And Briggs continued down Walton toward the noise and congestion and excitement and, he hoped, toward Linda Pastorini too.

2

WHEN GEORGIE BROUGHT Briggs to where Linda was stationed on the steps of the house on Walton Street, she didn't recognize him at first.

"The airport," Georgie said, turning and looking disgustedly at her out of the corner of his eye.

Briggs said, "You interviewed me."

"What do you want?"

"Do you know that interview's been shown every hour on the hour all morning?"

Did he expect to be paid? That didn't seem to be it. He stood there, hanging on to the strap of his shoulder bag, squinting at her. Fresh white shirt, tie off center, a gap between buttons where his shirt stretched over his pot, he wasn't what a girl dreamt of when she dreamt of a man. Unfortunately, he was par for the course, or so Linda thought.

"So what?"

"So what! I don't want to be mixed up in anything that's got to do with Iggie Moran."

"Then you shouldn't be here."

"I have an appointment at ten."

She couldn't figure him out. His complaint had to be an excuse. She remembered his pitch the night before. Good God, was he coming on to her?

"You worried about your wife?"

"Ha. You ought to be careful yourself, you know. Ask anyone about Iggie Moran."

"He's dead."

Briggs smiled tolerantly. He shifted gears. "Let's have lunch."

Georgie had hung around after bringing Briggs to her, and his eyebrows were dancing as he grinned leeringly at her. Maybe that's why she accepted.

"Where?"

"Got any suggestions?"

"The Palmer House. Noon?"

"Noon at the Palmer House."

She lit a cigarette and watched him go up the street, the shoulder bag bouncing off his hip. Was she really that hard up? But then the front door opened and the cops came out and she was swept up in her job, jostling with the other reporters, stretching to get a microphone in the face of Lieutenant Moriarity.

"Is Donna Moran staying here?"

"No."

"Aw, c'mon," yelled the *Sun-Times*, "what are you doing here then?"

"My sister lives here."

Moriarity obviously enjoyed giving the press a bad time and he devoted twenty minutes to it, parrying all questions, admitting nothing, denying less, having the time of his life. When he pushed past her Linda felt like jamming her microphone in his ear.

Georgie stashed the gear, and she called in and signed out. The Moran daughter was her story, so they rousted her out for the vigil on Walton Street but it had proved a dud.

"I'll drop you at your place," Georgie offered.

"I think I'll walk."

"It's hours till lunch."

"Go to hell."

"It's just as well. I'm parked two blocks north."

She started off south. Several hours spent standing on the steps of a more or less convent made her want to walk it off. Nuns. She had never understood nuns until she got married, but they didn't join up to get away from men, did they? How could they know how bad they really were?

She caught a glimpse of herself in a window and stopped. A boutique, women's clothes, but she studied her reflected self. Skin tight jeans, suede boots, open denim jacket and wine-colored sweater blouse. Her long straight hair had dried naturally after her morning shower. Dressed like that, she should be under thirty at least, who was she trying to kid? No wonder overweight middle-aged men sought her out, asked her to lunch. She decided she couldn't show up at the Palmer House dressed like this.

She turned from the window, and a man seated in a parked car, looking straight ahead, sent an irrational ripple of fear through her. Had she considered covering the Moran story dangerous before Briggs professed to be worried? A woman came out of the boutique and got into the car. The man behind the wheel was scarcely a threat, but he reminded her of last night, of the man Georgie had seen talking to Briggs at the cabstand.

"Why didn't you follow him?"

Georgie gave her one of his repertoire of disgusted looks. "Just run off and not tell you where I went?"

From the moment she heard the nun was missing, Linda kept thinking of that man who had taken off after the VW in which the nuns were riding. She looked up the street. No sign of Georgie. Linda walked back the way she had come, mounted the steps of the house where she had been keeping vigil, deserted of media now, and rang the bell.

The woman who answered the door was wearing a sweat

suit and there was the distinctive smell of cigarette smoke about her.

"I want to speak with the nuns."

"You're Linda Pastorini."

"Can I come in? I think I know something important about the missing nun."

"Weren't you here earlier with the rest of them?"

"Where are the sisters?"

"I'm Sister Joyce."

"Aw, come on."

"It's true."

Why would she lie? "My photographer saw a man follow your car from the airport last night."

"Come on in and tell Sister Mary Teresa."

Linda would have given anything to have Georgie there with his camera when she went into the study and saw the wizened little woman with the giant headdress at work at her desk. She nodded when Linda was announced but finished what she was writing before looking up.

"Cable News," the old nun said almost immediately. She looked at Joyce with disappointment. "I have nothing to say, my dear. I feel bad enough without having to talk about it."

"Linda saw something last night," Joyce said.

Looking into those clear blue eyes, Linda was glad she had not intended to lie. But the truth she had to tell seemed unimportant and trivial now, and the tone of her voice betrayed her sense that she was wasting this old nun's time. The clear blue eyes never left her.

"You've told the police, of course."

"No."

"Why not?"

"It just really dawned on me that it's important."

"Where is your photographer now?"

Linda wished she had gone straight home to change for her lunch with Briggs. She was a professional newswoman and she sounded like an idiot. Did she expect this old nun to saddle up and go looking for the man Briggs had directed after the VW last night?

"He'll go to the police," Linda promised. "In the meantime, I wanted to let you know . . ."

"That was good of you."

There was no sarcasm in the nun's voice, for which Linda was grateful.

"Well, I've got to go. You've had an awful morning."

A look of pain on the old face. "If I have I deserve it. Use the telephone. Call the photographer and tell him to inform the police. I cannot bear the thought of Sister Mary Magdalene . . ." But the old voice broke off, and her eyes filled with thoughts too horrible to voice. It was an odd sensation, being on the other side of a news story, seeing it from the perspective of the people involved, the people getting hurt.

Georgie had not yet returned to the station. Had he said he was going right back? Another younger nun came into the study while she was using the phone, Sister Kimberly.

"Call Richard, Sister," the old nun said. "Linda can tell him of the man who followed you last night."

Richard Moriarity was, it turned out, the young nun's brother. There was enough sarcasm in his voice for a dozen people. "Sister Mary Teresa put you up to this?"

"I'll have Georgie, my photographer, get in touch with you as soon as I reach him."

"I saw you at the house earlier. Why didn't you mention this then?"

"Look, Lieutenant, I'm trying to help. Maybe you don't need any help finding a kidnapped nun."

"If she's been kidnapped."

Linda couldn't believe the guy. Sister Kimberly took the phone but apparently Moriarity had hung up.

"He seemed to think I was kidding," Linda said in disbelief.

"Police are a skeptical breed," the old nun sighed, pushing back from her desk.

THREE

3

AFTER LINDA LEFT, Sister Mary Teresa remained standing, looking more anguished than Kim had ever seen her. It was silly to think that the old nun could just sit down and do her daily pages on the history of the twelfth century in these circumstances. It was bad enough that a guest had mysteriously disappeared, but for that guest to be the Carmelite nun who, Emtee Dempsey had assured her superior, would be as safe in Walton Street as in her Missouri convent, was an intolerable state of affairs.

"The police know nothing," she said, shaking her head.

"When they learn of the man who followed us from the airport . . ."

Emtee Dempsey was still shaking her head, causing her great headdress to sway, thus emphasizing the negative.

"Richard was skeptical and perhaps he is right. Even if there was such a man, how can they find him?"

"They will try."

Emtee Dempsey was not consoled. Usually she was quite willing to grant that Richard and his colleagues performed certain technical tasks as well as anyone could. Their deficiency was rather one of imagination and intelligence. It was the old nun's conceit that, given all that the police knew, any moderately intelligent person could discern the meaning of the facts, undeterred by the dulling conservatism of police routine. Well, perhaps not every moderately intelligent person. But most certainly Sister Mary Teresa Dempsey of the Order of Martha and Mary. The trouble with the present case, Kim observed, was that they knew as much as the police knew.

"Then we must learn more."

Joyce said, "You could ask Linda to bring her photographer here. It sounds like he'd be wasting his time with Richard anyway."

Kim half feared Emtee Dempsey would accept this advice. But her mind was on something else. She sat and looked at Kim.

"There are two Moran daughters."

It was enough for any moderately intelligent member of the Order of Martha and Mary to guess what was coming and, sure enough, the old nun wanted to speak with Lenore Moran. They knew the other sister was married, but none of them could come up with her married name. So Kim phoned Katherine Senski.

"Does Sister think that's where Donna Moran is?"

"Would you like to speak with her?"

"Aha," Katherine said. "So she's right at your elbow?"

Sister Mary Teresa looked up at Kim's apparent reference to her, but on the phone Katherine insisted that she would forego the privilege for the moment.

"Here it is, Lenore Cremona, née Moran. The address is in Oak Park."

●

Kim took Halstead to 290, which at a different hour of the day would sweep traffic back to the western suburbs. But now at two the freeway was relatively unused and she made it to her turn off at Austin in record time. The Cremonas lived in a large house on the border of Oak Park and River Forest. The Dominican nuns still operated their college in the neighborhood, and Kim felt a twinge of regret. What would her life have been like if the Order of Martha and Mary had not all but disappeared in the wake of the Second Vatican Council? She imagined days spent in the withdrawn, peaceful and regulated life of a real convent. She would have finished her degree long ago and been in the classroom, acquiring her own little entourage of students. Emtee Dempsey even now years afterward was the one to whom former students instinctively turned when their lives ran into trouble. Kim herself was still a member of that band, the students of Sister Emtee Dempsey, and she wouldn't have changed her life for the world. She did not rejoice that the order now consisted of the three of them on Walton Street, but given that fact she liked her life. For one thing she was often sent on wild goose chases like the present one.

"Bring her to see me if she'll come," Emtee Dempsey said. It was difficult to know what the old nun's image of the outside world was. Did she have any idea of the distance between Oak Park and Walton Street or that Lenore Cremona might be in no mood to talk with her? Her family had become the talk of the town since her brother's suit against the archdiocese, and now her sister the Carmelite was missing. Driving slowly up the avenue on which the Cremonas lived, hunched forward to read the numbers of the houses, Kim could not quell the irrational hope that she would find Sister Mary Magdalene safely with her sister.

Lenore Cremona was in her way as otherworldly as her sister the nun. Dark hair parted in the middle hung lankly to frame a narrow, dramatic face, the face of an El Greco Madonna. She was holding one baby while another child clung to her skirt, and her expression might have been the one with which she accepted each new twist in her fate. Except that Kim did not quite believe that Lenore was the tied-down housewife she seemed. There was no sign of resignation in the large liquid eyes she turned on Kim.

"I'm Sister Kimberly, Mrs. Cremona. May I come in?"

"Sister?"

"Donna was staying with us."

"Oh, my God." The expression was ambiguous, a prayer, a curse, neither. She had looked incredulous when Kim identified herself as a nun and now she drew herself straight.

"I wish Joe was here."

The child clinging to her mother's skirt began to cry, and Kim stooped and took her into her arms, an uncalculated move, but it gained her entry to the house. The large living room might have been moved intact from a furniture store window. A walkway of wrapping paper led from the front door to the kitchen.

The kitchen at least looked lived in; maybe it was where Lenore and her children spent most of their time.

"I'm drinking Coke," Lenore said. She had taken a chair at the table and now lifted a glass. Her expression responded to Kim's. "I drink it all the time."

"No thanks."

"I could make coffee."

Kim shook her head and sat across from Lenore.

"Have you heard from Donna?"

She sipped from her glass, the baby on her lap following the action. "Is she really missing?"

"Yes."

"I thought it was a trick of Randy's. What a fool he was to start all this."

"All this" was her brother's suit against the archdiocese, but she could scarcely blame him for the prosecutor's activities. Wiley was out to harm the Moran name while her brother, however mixed and crude his methods, claimed to be protecting the family honor. Lenore said that her only wish was to live anonymously in Oak Park, taking care of her house, raising her children, cooking for Joe.

"Not that he has much of an appetite. I've learned to cook Italian but it doesn't matter, he eats like a bird."

She spoke of her husband as if he were one of her children. If she was worried about her missing sister she did not show it.

"How long has it been since you saw Donna?"

A shrug. "Since she went away to become a nun, I guess."

"How long is that?"

She looked across the room to where the oldest child leaned against a counter and followed the conversation at the table. "Julia is four." She shook her head. "It can't be ten years. Eight?"

"Were you close?"

"Donna and me?" She seemed to find the suggestion strange. "I guess we were, in a way. She's two years younger than I am. People sometimes thought we were twins, but we're totally different. Except for looks. Then. You've seen her?"

"I picked her up at the airport. I saw her this morning. Lenore, I'm here to ask if you have any idea what might have happened to her."

"Me!"

"Some people suggest themselves right off, of course. Why do you think your brother would kidnap Donna?"

"Isn't she here because he's suing the cardinal?"

"But on what side?"

Lenore thought a moment, then shook her head. "Donna would never do anything to hurt the family."

"Have you talked with your brother?"

"No! All we want to do is live our lives like everyone else. Why did Randy have to stir all this up again? If this is his way of expressing loyalty to the family, he's crazy." Her voice rose as she spoke, and it would have been impossible not to feel sympathy with her. Kim felt that she had only added to the woman's troubles by coming here, but of course that was Emtee Dempsey's fault. The old nun's notion that Lenore might be persuaded to come talk with her in the study on Walton Street seemed fantastic sitting at this suburban kitchen table with a harried mother and two children needing constant attention. As if to exonerate herself, Kim began to tell Lenore about Sister Mary Teresa.

"Oh, I met her once! What a character. She was Donna's teacher."

"Sister would love to talk to you now."

"Now?"

"She hoped I could persuade you to visit her in our house on Walton Street."

A delighted expression faded quickly. "She thinks I know where Donna is."

"She thinks you may know things that would help find your sister, things you don't even know you know."

"I can't imagine what they would be."

"We could take the children."

Was it the prospect of getting out of the house, of having help with the children when she did, that altered Lenore's attitude? Kim correctly read the change of expression on Lenore Cremona's face and got to her feet.

"Where are the children's wraps?"

All resistance fled when the oldest child responded to the prospect of going out.

And so, at ten-thirty, less than an hour after having turned up at the Cremona door, Kim was on her way back to Walton Street with the baby in her car seat in the back of the VW and little Julia on her mother's lap in the passenger seat beside her.

THE PHONE WAS ringing when Linda stepped from the shower, but by the time she got to it the ringing stopped. She tried to feel relief, calls were usually a nuisance, but it was worse to stand there wondering who it had been. Her number was unlisted, so it should be possible to guess. Someone from the station? For all she knew, the phone had been ringing all the while she was in the shower. She was on her way back to the bathroom when the ringing began again. This time she got it.

"Yes?"

"Linda Pastorini?"

"Who's calling?"

"Lieutenant Moriarity. I want to talk to you."

"So talk."

"You busy at the moment?"

To tell him she had just stepped from the shower might sound provocative. Georgie, when she mentioned the lieutenant's good looks, had told her the man was married. Well, so had her husbands been, but she'd had no illusions about them.

"Is this official or unofficial?"

A pause. "Official."

"Then we can do it on the phone."

He had talked with Georgie and been told of the salesman Briggs as the only one who would have gotten a good look at the man who had followed Donna Moran from the airport.

"A fat little guy, as Georgie described him. But he said you'd know more about him."

Linda was in a spot. She was getting ready to meet Briggs for lunch at the Palmer House and was reluctant to tell the handsome Lieutenant Moriarity this. What would he think of her standards?

"Georgie saw him as well as I did. Besides, he's on the clip we ran, if you want a good look. Georgie should have told you that."

"He did. He also said Briggs came down to Walton Street this morning."

Damn you, Georgie. "He was angry we put him on the tube."

"Why angry?"

"He said he feared Iggie Moran even if he was dead."

"You believe him?"

"I'm just telling you what he said."

"He threaten you in any way?"

"Briggs?" She laughed. Too late, she saw she was missing an opportunity. "I'm used to threats."

"Oh?"

"I've been married twice."

"Briggs say where he was staying?"

"You ought to be able to find that out."

"Do me a favor. If he gets in touch with you, let me know."

"Why would he get in touch with me?"

"To threaten you."

Funny. She hung up and went to dress, feeling disloyal to Briggs for the way she had dismissed him. Maybe she was getting too desperate. A man like Moriarity was more her style. The trouble was, men like that were usually married. Maybe Briggs was married too.

She had returned to her apartment and showered with a sense of anticipation, but by the time she left for the Palmer House all sense of adventure was gone. Briggs seemed an obstacle between her and such men as Moriarity rather than the acceptable port in a storm he had seemed that morning on Walton Street.

It was twenty after twelve when she got out of the cab at the Palmer House. She took the escalator to the lobby and crossed to the entrance of the restaurant. Briggs was not visible, but no doubt he had taken a table to wait for her in comfort.

"Mr. Briggs's table," she told the haughty hostess.

"Briggs." A slight frown as she scanned the large open book. She glanced at Linda. "You said Briggs. With a B."

There was no Briggs with a B on the hostess's list. Not only was she here first, he hadn't even made a reservation, and by the looks of the restaurant that meant they would have a nice long wait when he finally got here.

Linda went back to the lobby and sat in the smoking area where, after a moment's thought, she decided to take up smoking. She had quit for good an hour and a half before, but it seemed a shame not to make use of an area set aside for smokers. Besides, the cigarette gave her something to do while she waited. Time passed, she lit another cigarette, if only to have company in her smoldering. Had he forgotten? She reviewed the exchange on Walton Street, trying to discover in the memory an indication that he might have been kidding, but she was certain he'd been serious. He liked her. She had sensed that last night at the airport, it was even more obvious this morning. He had been delayed, that was all. She would give him hell when he showed up late, and that was the best appetizer of all. But the scarcely admitted thoughts while she showered were definitely shelved. There wasn't a chance in the world she and Briggs would check in and go up to a room and join battle against loneliness.

At one o'clock she told herself he wasn't coming. For whatever reason, he had stood her up. She stayed until one-thirty, just in case. In part it was her unwillingness to believe that she had sunk to the point where she was jilted by men like B. G. Briggs. In part it was because she really had nothing else to do. She might have gone in and had lunch alone, but that would have made her plight seem more pathetic still.

From a phone booth that gave her a view of the lobby, she called the station, if only to give her the sense that her life retained some purpose. Damn Briggs. Georgie wasn't in. She tried his cellular phone and got him.

"You home, Linda?"

"I'm downtown."

"Where? I'll pick you up." An interval during which she heard the noise of traffic. "It's important."

As she went down to street level, she half feared she'd run into the tardy Briggs. It would be some small satisfaction to tell the bastard off. But then it was better not to let him know it mattered. Georgie, bless his heart, was double-parked outside when she emerged onto the street.

"Why did you tell Moriarity to call me?" she asked, punching his arm as he pulled away.

"They found Briggs."

"Found him!"

"Dead."

An involuntary cry escaped her. For nearly two hours she had been angry with a dead man. Maybe that was the best way to get unsettling news, weaving through traffic, with a maniacal driver like Georgie at the wheel, only half attending to the other cars as he told her of the discovery of the bullet-riddled body of B. G. Briggs.

5

THE FRENETIC JOURNEY across town with Lenore and her kids might have convinced Kim she did indeed have a religious vocation if she'd had any doubt about it before. How did parents summon the patience and self-denial kids demand? Lenore's ability to coddle and soothe her baby while keeping up an unbroken conversation with Kim seemed a superhuman feat. It was clear that Lenore had precisely the life she wanted, a husband, children, a home in which she was the central figure. That was why she was so upset by the recent turn of events—Wiley, the prosecutor, resurrecting her father's alleged crimes, her brother initiating a lawsuit against the archdiocese that had been lovingly covered in all the papers, a sister brought back from her convent in Missouri only to disappear, apparently kidnapped, thereby increasing the intensity of interest in the Moran family.

Julia had managed to undo the buckle of the seat belt and Kim steered with one hand as she tried unsuccessfully to refasten it. Was it this constant concern for her children that explained Lenore's absence of any visible anxiety about the fate of her sister?

The children were rendered mute by the sight of Sister Mary Teresa, but by talking to Kim and as it were inadvertently patting heads, rumpling hair, tugging them against her, the old nun soon overcame their apprehension.

"You are the first member of the family to whom I can express my utter dismay that your sister should be missing from this house," Sister Mary Teresa said to Lenore. "I doubt she would have come to Chicago at all if I had not convinced her superior that she would be safe as could be with us."

"It's awful to say, Sister, but one of the nicest things about getting married is that my name was no longer Moran. All my life I'd been aware of Daddy's reputation but it was like a dirty rumor at school or on the news, we never spoke of it at home. And then I became Mrs. Joseph Cremona and all that was behind me. And it was, until now. Donna should have stayed in Missouri."

"At the moment, I am inclined to agree with you. Who do you think took her?"

Lenore cast a glance at Kim. "Why would you think I'd know a thing like that? I haven't seen Donna in years. She writes twice a year. If my husband didn't answer I'm not sure that I would. It's as if we used to be sisters but it doesn't matter anymore. She's a nun way off in Missouri, I have my life, my home and family."

"It's not recent times that interest me, Mrs. Cremona. Just now it's easy to imagine that your brother or someone acting in his interests took Donna away. They thought she was going to testify against her father's memory."

"Donna would never do that." Lenore spoke with absolute certainty.

"No, I don't suppose a daughter would turn against her father."

Lenore shook her head. "It was more than that. Donna tried to ignore what she knew about Daddy and Marilyn Derecho. Finally she couldn't kid herself any longer. That's why she went into the convent."

"I don't understand."

"To do penance. For Daddy. To save his soul. I guess it worked."

Emtee Dempsey was seldom without words, but she observed a moment of silence after this. Lenore shifted the baby on her lap. "That helped Joe to make up his mind too, so I should be grateful too."

"Tell me about that."

What woman does not enjoy telling of the way she came to marry the man she did? Joe had been interested in the two sisters, but as so often happens, the sister who liked him was not the one he preferred. He wasn't handsome in a conventional sense and he was a diabetic. Lenore mentioned these things as if they were pluses, all the more reason to love Joe.

"Joe hadn't been to college and of course Donna graduated from yours. It wouldn't have worked, as he came to see. But it helped that Donna went into the convent."

"He was her only beau?

"Oh, no. There was Marilyn's brother."

"Marilyn Derecho?"

"Uh-huh. Her brother Alan."

"And how did he react to his sister's having an affair with your father?"

Lenore winced and lifted her shoulders as if in protection against this charge. "He once tried to kill Daddy."

"What?"

"It never became public, Daddy saw to that. Alan tried to run Daddy down but missed and jumped the sidewalk and drove right into a boutique, terrifying everybody. Alan was knocked out by the impact and was in a coma for days. That was when my father had a friend testify that Alan had swerved to miss a madman driving on the wrong side of the road. Alan regained consciousness to find he was regarded as a hero."

"And what's become of Alan Derecho?"

"He stopped being a hero, that's for sure."

Alan Derecho had become an alcoholic and there had been

other incidents with automobiles in which no one considered him a hero. He had spent a significant fraction of his life in therapy, being dried out but returning to ordinary life like someone who had lost the knack of walking and couldn't help seeming out of step. A few years ago he opened a business on the near North Side.

"What kind of business?"

"Women's wear. Joe is sure Alan is the one who stirred up the prosecutor."

"Vengeance for his sister?"

"I guess."

"I wish your husband was here for our talk."

"What time is it?"

Emtee Dempsey fished a watch out from under her wimple, pressed the stem and it flew open. It was going on four o'clock.

"I'll call and have him pick us up. He finishes work at four-thirty."

"Where does he work?"

"Midstate Paper."

She made the call and Joyce served cocoa in the kitchen where they were all still chatting when the door bell rang. Joe Cremona had come for his family. He was a surprise, a head shorter than Lenore, swarthy, his proletarian air unaltered by the suit and tie he wore. He was, it emerged, vice president in charge of sales at Midstate Paper. It was Lenore who told them this, her voice vibrant with pride.

"Did you eat a big lunch?" Lenore asked.

"I'm all right."

"Could Joe have cocoa, Sister?"

Lenore's concern was generated by her husband's diabetes. If his blood sugar sank he could go into a coma. Joe was visibly uncomfortable in these nunnish surroundings, and responded in monosyllables when Emtee Dempsey addressed him. Until she mentioned Alan Derecho.

"That bastard! Whoops. I'm sorry." And he covered his mouth with his hand, looking to Lenore for help.

"I've told them all about Alan."

"The Derechos seem to be an unfortunate family," Emtee Dempsey observed.

"Like the Morans," said Lenore.

SIX

THE NAME MILDRED Scott did not at first mean anything to Katherine but she told her secretary to send the woman in. Of course she recognized the actress from her appearances on television after she had misled the media and permitted Donna Moran to get safely, as it had seemed, to the house on Walton Street.

"I'm told you're a friend of Sister Mary Teresa," Mildred Scott said, standing before Katherine's desk despite the invitation to be seated. She had a beret tugged rakishly forward, obscuring one eye, and was wrapped in a monk's cloth cloak that Katherine envied. "I betrayed her."

"I wish you'd sit down. Let me take your wrap."

Mildred unwound from her cape in a practiced manner. She was clad in a velvet siren suit tucked into boots. Katherine, a flamboyant dresser herself, felt drab and uninspired in the presence of Mildred.

"Where did you get this cape?"

"A gift." A sad faraway look. "But I don't want to get started on *him*."

"I'm surprised you were persuaded to disguise yourself as a nun."

"Of course it was a challenge. And for a good cause. But in my weakness I could not forego turning it to personal advantage as well. As soon as the real nun was safe at her destination, I felt it perfectly kosher to exploit the situation on my own behalf. An actress can never get too much publicity. Now I feel responsible for her kidnapping."

Doubtless Mildred saw further possibilities for free publicity in the role she had played. The kidnapping of the Carmelite kept the story alive and, sure enough, Mildred had come to the Tribune Tower in order to speak to a reporter. From a higher viewpoint, it might have been good for Katherine's soul to realize that the actress had not come specifically to see her. As it was, she was irked to learn that the mention of Sister Mary Teresa Dempsey had provided young Fraggert with an excuse to send Mildred on to Katherine Senski. For which, though she would never admit it to Fraggert, Katherine thanked God.

"You were the one who alerted the media that Donna Moran was returning to Chicago, weren't you?"

"That's what I'm saying. I had perfect confidence in my ability to carry off the ruse I'd been hired to do. The idea, you must know, was Sister Mary Teresa's. I wonder if she realizes how few actresses would have been able to make the plan work."

"I am sure she is impressed with your talents."

Mildred seated herself and crossed one velvet leg over the other. "Do you mind if I smoke?"

"Tobacco?"

Half a second of incomprehension, and then Mildred's eyes sparked with appreciation. "Don't be misled, Miss Senski," she said as she shook a cigarette free from her package. "Like most people in the theater I live a comparatively conservative life."

"Except for the occasional gift of a cloak?"

Mildred's eyes closed and her brows lifted. "Suffering is

good for an actress. Real suffering. Only the wounded can respond to the variety of human experience."

"Donna Moran was followed from O'Hare to the house on Walton Street. Whom did you tell other than the media?"

Even to ask the question was to realize its stupidity. Mildred had told enough people who might have told someone else and thus eventually the word got to those who kidnapped Donna Moran.

Mildred sat forward. "Is that how you think it happened?"

"Don't you?"

"Oh, I hope you're right. I had thought it was my explaining the trick the following day that led the kidnappers to the nun's residence. But if it was someone else who told, I'm not guilty. And it had to be, didn't it? The poor thing was already gone before I acknowledged that it was I who had met the press at O'Hare." She sighed. "I can't tell you how I have been blaming myself."

"And rightly so, since you must have told the person through whom word got to the kidnappers."

But Mildred was uninterested in trickle-down guilt. If she was deprived of the opportunity to take full and solitary blame, she regarded herself as innocent as the driven snow.

"Who kidnapped her, Miss Senski?"

"Call me Katherine. I don't know."

"Her brother?"

That suggestion was so obvious, Katherine had simply dismissed it, but perhaps she was being overly sophisticated. Why not think the obvious person had taken Donna away from Walton Street? Randy Moran had the best motive of all. He wanted to prevent Donna from providing what he clearly thought would be damaging testimony against their father.

"You may be right."

"You sound doubtful."

"That is an idea the police will have been pursuing. If there were anything to it I think we would know by now."

To make sure, she checked to see what the latest on Donna

71

Moran was. Her great dread was that she would be told the body of the Carmelite nun had been found. She herself could keep busy at the *Tribune*, but poor Emtee Dempsey would find it more difficult to distract herself from what must appear to her to be her unworthy stewardship. Katherine knew the confidence with which Sister Mary Teresa had assured the Carmelite superior in Missouri that Donna Moran could stay with them in an atmosphere indistinguishable from that she would know in her home convent.

It was difficult to believe that any other convent was as lively a place as the house on Walton Street. There were days when Katherine secretly rejoiced that Sister Mary Teresa and herself, as a member of the board of trustees, had lost their battle to preserve the M&M college. The dissolution of the Order of Martha and Mary had seemed an unmitigated disaster at the time, and it particularly pained Katherine to think that a place to which she was linked by so many personal memories could actually cease to exist. Somehow the death of an institution seemed more tragic than the death of an individual. Was it possible that she would no longer be able to visit her old friend and spend hours in conversation, surrounded by the scenes and buildings where the two of them had been young girls? In any event, the move to Walton Street had made Emtee Dempsey far more accessible. No need to worry that the old nun would be unable to adapt to radically altered circumstances. Together with the two young nuns she lived as regular a life as was possible in a house situated in the very midst of urban distractions. That house on Walton had become for Katherine a redoubt of peace and nostalgia.

There was nothing new on Donna Moran.

"Did you check the morgue?"

There was a pause on the line and then Fraggert said, "You're serious."

"Let me know."

Mildred Scott waited patiently for Katherine to complete the call much as, on stage, she would await the cue for her own

72

lines, not really interested in what the other actors said or did.

"Katherine, I came to ask you to be my intercessor with Sister Mary Teresa. How I admire that woman! In her presence, for the first time, I was able to imagine what it must be like to be a nun. I mean in the traditional sense. These latter day so-called nuns, ordinary clothes, maybe a veil, are something else. But a complete withdrawal from the world, signaled by a distinctive garb, a peaceful regulated life, ah . . ."

Katherine did not stop her. She too was sometimes visited by such thoughts, but it was not really easy to imagine even the life on Walton Street as one she herself could live. As a girl she had felt a fleeting attraction to the convent, most Catholic girls did, but it had not been difficult to overcome it, even when her best friend became Sister Mary Teresa.

"I want her to know how abject I am. I want to know if I can come see her again."

Mischievously, Katherine asked, "Do you want me to tell her about your attraction to the convent?"

Mildred was startled. "That isn't what I meant."

Fraggert stood in the doorway, staring at Katherine, ignoring Mildred Scott. Katherine felt a chill pass over her. Involuntarily, her hands came together in prayer.

"You called the morgue?"

He nodded.

"Well?"

"Remember that salesman, Briggs, the one interviewed at the airport?"

"No."

"Linda Pastorini interviewed him on TV."

"What about him?"

"He's dead. His body's in the morgue. I guess you can say he's connected with the Donna Moran disappearance."

SEVEN

L INDA PASTORINI HAD attended four years of grade school taught by nuns in a parish in western Pennsylvania, but her memories of the experience were vague. She would have been unable to draw a picture of the garb those nuns wore if she had been asked. What stayed with her was a mood, an atmosphere, rather than images, and the mood was one of serenity and peace. The Pastorini household had been a hectic place where turbulent emotions and scarcely repressed violence were the order of the day. To imagine her parents as lovers would have been impossible, yet they were gruffly affectionate, and all the little Pastorinis testified to something. But serene and peaceful they were not. In the animal kingdom mating often seems to occur when the female has lost a physical struggle. Linda thought of herself and her siblings as tokens of paternal victory over maternal reluctance.

No doubt her own marriages had been affected by that past, her notion of the relation between man and woman formed, however unwillingly, on the model of her battling parents. It occurred to her that she had picked husbands who could not dominate her. BGB fell into that pattern, didn't he? Safe and ineffectual, an instrument of her fantasies, basically unserious. And now he was dead.

It was difficult to mourn a man she had not really known. They had had two conversations, that was all, the second because she had manipulated him in the first. She had been inclined to dismiss his expression of fear when he came to Walton Street that morning as phony, a ploy to talk with her again, but something of his own apprehension must have stuck to her. Not that that explained why she had agreed to meet him at the Palmer House. After she accepted, she had watched him walk away, a dumpy middle-aged figure, a man who obviously smoked and drank and ate too much, probably a ticking bomb healthwise because of the way he lived. What were her feelings as she watched that receding figure, his upper body wider because of the shoulder bag he carried? It didn't seem too much to call it affection, a sense of being somehow in the same boat as BGB. And, after all, later in the shower she'd entertained vague thoughts of adjourning to a room after their lunch and doing what salesmen do when they are on the road. And now B. G. Briggs was dead.

Georgie chattered away about it as he might any trivial item of the news, the way she herself reported on disaster, tragedy, famine and fire, a daily diet of such bad news hardening her to the fact that human beings exactly like herself were caught up in them. Why should Georgie react differently to the death of Briggs? There was something monstrous in this matter-of-fact acceptance of the misfortunes of others. She looked at Georgie, huddled over the wheel, talking a mile a minute and trying to drive at the same rate. Did she get along with Georgie too because he was no threat at all? He became aware of her stare and observed a second of silence before asking, "What were you doing at the Palmer House?"

"Waiting for Briggs."

A glance. "Not funny."

"I'm serious. We had a date for lunch."

Georgie's mouth dropped open and he eased into a slower lane. They were snaking along Lake Shore Drive as she had suggested. "My God! I forgot."

"I've been waiting there since shortly after noon. Can you believe it? Waiting several hours for Briggs?"

"Where we going?"

"Walton Street."

"What for?"

Good question. Linda wanted to talk to Sister Mary Teresa. She felt she should be called into the principal's office to explain herself. Of course it was absurd to think that because she had been waiting for Briggs she was somehow responsible for his death, but from the moment she heard the news from Georgie, Linda had been certain those events at O'Hare explained what had happened to Briggs. The salesman had been unlucky enough to point out Donna Moran to the kidnapper. With Briggs out of the way, there was no one to identify the kidnapper.

"Except maybe you."

"Me!" Georgie involuntarily stepped on the gas and nearly tailgated the car ahead of them.

"There must have been more than one. One man talks to Briggs and goes sprinting off after the VW, right? You think he picks up his car along the way and then goes in pursuit. By then he would have lost them. Another person could have been parked short of the entrance and taken off after him but not before seeing you talking with Briggs."

"For chrissake, cut it out, will you? Nobody saw me. I couldn't identify the guy who talked with Briggs."

"They sound like very tidy people to me. You might seem a loose string."

It was cruel teasing Georgie, but Linda half believed the little photographer was in trouble. In any case her speculation drowned out any unwillingness he had to stop in at Walton Street. Linda's excuse, formulated on the way, was that she wanted the old nun's reaction to this new turn of events involving the visit to Chicago of the former Donna Moran, now Sister Mary Magdalene of the Carmelite Order.

THREE

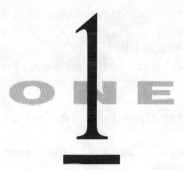

ONE

KIM WAS IN the study with Richard and Emtee Dempsey when Joyce peeked around the door and gave her a significant look. Kim excused herself and followed Joyce down the hall to the kitchen, where Linda Pastorini and a little fellow with an action camera sat at the table with mugs of coffee before them.

"They want to see Sister Mary Teresa," Joyce whispered. "I told them Richard was with her."

"There's been a new development."

"Briggs? Linda Pastorini asked.

The newswoman looked all dolled up, different than she had that morning, but her expression did not go with her outfit.

"Of course you would know. We do because my brother is convinced we aren't telling him everything we know, and he thinks the death of this man should convince us something serious is going on. He is very wrong to think Sister Mary Teresa takes lightly the kidnapping of a guest from this house. How could she ignore what might have happened to our missing guest?"

"Briggs stood Linda up," the photographer said.

"We were supposed to have lunch at the Palmer House. He said he had a ten o'clock appointment. Anyway, he didn't show up."

Kim didn't know what to say to that, but Joyce saved the day.

"Haven't you had lunch?"

Linda hadn't and Joyce went into action, preparing omelets for both the newspeople. They were eating when Richard looked in.

"I wondered where you'd gone. Are you giving interviews yet?"

"What's the latest on Briggs?" Linda asked.

"Check the morgue."

"Who shot him?"

"You'll be the first to know."

"Meaning you don't."

Richard asked Kim to return to the study with him. "I want you to talk some sense into her," he said audibly as they went down the hall.

There were times when Kim wondered how her brother had advanced as far as he had in his chosen profession. He'd certainly known Sister Mary Teresa long enough to know that she was far too sensible to have sense talked into her by anyone. Admittedly, she could be irritating and whimsical and, on occasion, if only in the short term, flat-out wrong, but somehow her grasp of events turned out to be unfailing. So Kim was not surprised when Emtee Dempsey asked Richard if the prime suspect in the death of B. G. Briggs was Randy Moran.

"I believe you suggested earlier that he was the one who had kidnapped his sister."

"Have you satisfied yourself that he did not?" Emtee Dempsey asked.

"Everything he says he was doing for the past couple days turns out to be true."

"No doubt. Surely you didn't expect him personally to

82

abscond with his sister. And by the by, that was your idea, not mine. I did not contradict you, of course, but I would not wish to rob you of your intuitions."

"Intuitions!" Richard made a face. "Are you suggesting that he kidnapped his sister?"

"I am suggesting that you pursue that line of inquiry."

Richard was mollified when Emtee Dempsey became docile and asked him what was known of the circumstances of Briggs's death. The man had been a salesman who worked out of St. Louis, representing F. X. Nicolo Creations of Milan. American headquarters for the company were in Chicago, and Briggs made frequent flights to the city. He had flown into Chicago last night on the plane that brought Donna Moran to O'Hare. One passenger thought Briggs might have helped the Carmelite get past the waiting newsmen. But it was doubtful this would have been possible without the diversion staged by Mildred Scott.

"Your employee," Richard said darkly.

"She did a good deal more than I asked her to do. There would have been no newspeople there if Mildred hadn't alerted them. She wanted an audience to work to."

"You should talk, with a crew from Cable News in your kitchen."

Why when she was genuinely surprised did Emtee Dempsey seem least convincing? Kim could forgive Richard for thinking the old nun was relying on one of her many morally okay ways of deceiving him when she assured him that it was news to her that Linda Pastorini and her photographer were in the house.

"Bring them in," she said to Kim.

The fact that Linda had been waiting for Briggs at the Palmer House where he had arranged to meet her after a ten o'clock appointment was added to his dossier on the dead salesman.

"Did he say who the appointment was with?"

"No. I hope he kept that one."

"Are you so sure?" Emtee Dempsey asked, and Linda's eyes grew large.

Richard rose. "Well, back to the missing Carmelite. I must run out and arrest Randy Moran. Any other suggestions?"

"Do keep me posted on events."

"You'll continue to be the first to know."

Georgie had stayed in the kitchen with Joyce, preferring the known evil, as he ambiguously suggested, and Kim was immediately struck by the lack of urgency in Linda's manner as she sat in a chair across from Emtee Dempsey's desk. Kim remarked on the fact that Linda had been waiting for Briggs at a restaurant when she learned that he was dead.

"How awful for you."

"How awful for him."

"God rest his soul."

"I went to school with the nuns when I was a girl, in Pennsylvania."

"What order were they?"

"I don't know. I don't think I even suspected there were different kinds of nun."

Far from being an opening gambit, it turned out to be what Linda Pastorini wanted to talk about, and Emtee Dempsey, as if she hadn't a thing to do in the world, chattered on with the newswoman, pouring the tea Kim brought in on a tray, eventually turning the conversation to Linda's career.

"Calling it a career makes it sound far grander than it is, Sister. Most days I envy women who can stay home all day. Today I'm envying nuns."

"Maybe you have a vocation."

"I've been married twice."

"Well, that takes care of purgatory."

It was good to hear Linda's husky laughter.

When Linda realized that she had spent over an hour with them, she rose in a panic. "Speaking of my career. Would you let me interview you, Sister?"

"So I can broadcast to the world the fact that young nuns are not safe in my keeping?" One of the most painful experiences of the old nun's life had been the call to Missouri when she informed Sister Mary Magdalene's superior that the young nun was missing. She could not bring herself to use the term kidnap. She professed to be most unnerved by the calmness with which the news was received. The lack of a reproach was the worst reproach of all.

"Let me ask Georgie in here."

Georgie's expression when he first laid eyes on Sister Mary Teresa would have been far more worthy of taping than the interview that followed, so Kim disloyally thought. Actually, the interview was a virtuoso performance, on both Linda's and Emtee Dempsey's part. Their earlier conversation had broken the ice between them and established an easy give-and-take that lent the interview an easy authority.

"I will leave to the consciences of public officials the wisdom of raking up the alleged misbehavior of departed citizens," Emtee Dempsey said, frowning sternly at the lens of Georgie's camera. "It is a biblical truth that the sins of fathers are visited on their children, but I rather doubt that the city government intends to abide by all scriptural admonitions and observations. Now that a member of a once-prominent family has come into harm's way because of the questionable zeal of the prosecutor's office, we may no doubt expect public expression of regret for the proposed legal harassment of the family. If Sister Mary Magdalene is permitted to hear my words let me say to her that she is constantly in our prayers and that we shall not rest until she is back under this roof. I made a solemn promise to her superior that she would be safe with me, and I now stand convicted of misleading her and all the members of Sister Mary Magdalene's community. I have little doubt that many dark deeds must be played out before these matters are put to rest. The prosecutor has started a chain of events from which there is no easy escape now."

"That was pretty pessimistic," Linda said as she and Georgie prepared to leave.

"Look after yourselves."

And Linda and Georgie looked at each other and then back at the old nun.

"Maybe we should ask for sanctuary here."

"If only it could be called that, Linda," the old nun said, and her voice was heavy with sadness.

2

TWO

KATHERINE SENSKI HAD pondered the message from the time she received it. *Sister Mary Magdalene is no more.* Her hope had been that by rushing to Sister Mary Teresa with it, something could be done at once. Now three days later, what struck her was that despite the ominous message everyone continued to speak in terms of a kidnapping. That there had been a kidnapping seemed true enough, but the message suggested that had been preliminary to a grimmer intent. In the still of the night, watching the shadows race across her ceiling, Katherine wondered if the body of the young nun lay moldering somewhere in the Chicago area while the living continued to fuss about her disappearance. Not that she imagined that the mere presence of a dead body would alter things. After all, there was the body of Briggs, of the Gold Coast Jeweler Skelly, and God knew how many others defying explanation. The difference with Donna was that she was a nun and the daughter of Iggie Moran.

Katherine's long journalistic jousting with Iggie Moran, the deep-seated contempt she had felt for the man, her long and successful effort to resist the blarney and charm that had won over otherwise sane folk, made her oddly more sympathetic to the man's daughter. Of course she imagined that Donna had gotten herself to a nunnery to do penance for her father. Imagine a man who would make a mistress out of his daughter's best friend! For Donna, that must have been the unkindest cut of all. And of course it had been a fateful move for Marilyn Derecho.

Marilyn had by all accounts been genuinely gifted. Prima facie, one suspected that Iggie would have greased her way through law school, but this proved not to be true. Of course Iggie could not have landed her a position in the top drawer law firm that hired her when she graduated from Northwestern Law. Why would a beautiful and intelligent young woman fall prey to such an odious person as Iggie Moran? The answer seemed to be drugs, and that fact conjured up the dark days of the white slave traffic. Had Iggie made Marilyn beholden to him through addiction? Katherine found this hypothesis as good as any other. What was more difficult to remember with equanimity was Iggie's predeathbed conversion. Good Catholic that she was, Katherine could not consciously wish ill to Iggie alive, let alone dead. She had often thrilled with Catholic horror when Hamlet, finding his hated uncle at prayer, put off slaying him, not wishing the man to die while in the act of addressing himself to God and thus presumably in a state of grace. Better to find him in the act of sin and dispatch him to eternal punishment. Christians had perhaps become flabby and sentimental about the Last Things. Katherine herself was sometimes tempted to think of eternal punishment as a pardonable imaginative excess by Dante and others, but her wavering faith was strengthened by Emtee Dempsey.

"Katherine, it would make a mockery of human freedom if, no matter how we use or abuse it, we are all ultimately to be rewarded."

"But how can a good God send anyone to hell?"

"He cannot. He does not. He does, however, acquiesce in the creature's free choice to separate himself forever from the sole point of his existence. This is not speculation. It is God himself who tells us this. And he ought to know."

Nonetheless, Katherine had been peeved by the sight of Iggie kneeling at the side of his long-suffering wife, conspicuous in a front pew, a daily communicant at last. So it was that she set about her investigative tasks, torn between contempt for the father and anguished concern for the daughter. She was employed by the *Tribune,* she was engaged in research for her stories, but at the same time she felt she was gathering information that, in the hands of Sister Mary Teresa, would cast light on the sad events of the past several days.

The death of B. G. Briggs, the ladies garment salesman from St. Louis, flared into newsworthiness, flickered and went out. He had spent the night before his death at the Stevenson, indeed he was still registered there at the time of his death. The police had taken custody of his luggage. He had been seen on Walton Street at the media stakeout and there complained to Linda Pastorini about the fact that his face had appeared on television in connection with the return of Iggie Moran's daughter to Chicago. No mention was made of the luncheon date he had made with Linda, nor that he had left to keep a ten o'clock appointment. He had expressed fear of Iggie dead or alive. That had seemed promising at first, suggestive of some past link of Briggs and Moran, perhaps some connection between Briggs and the missing Donna Moran, but nothing had been turned up in St. Louis or Chicago to justify this. Briggs had visited Chicago twice a month for years, but was in and out of the city in a matter of days. Since it was lacking in the newspaper account, it came as a surprise to Katherine that Linda Pastorini had accepted an invitation to have lunch with Briggs. Why?

"Perhaps she wanted to have lunch," Emtee Dempsey said.

Katherine smiled. On Walton Street it was assumed that she was the one wise in the ways of men and women, but the truth was she was as baffled as anyone else by the pairs people formed. Linda and Briggs were no odder couple than thousands of others. In any case, the old nun dismissed the matter.

"I want to know about Alan Derecho."

Of course! There would be a twisted symmetry if the brother of the dead Marilyn should avenge his sister by taking the life of the Moran daughter who had been her friend. But this required a version of Alan Derecho that did not match Katherine's memories.

"He is what is currently called a wimp, Sister. Besides, he and Marilyn were not close. To put it gently, since striking out with Donna Moran he's had as little to do with women as he could."

"Does he have an occupation?"

"He has a business on the North Side."

"What does he sell?"

"Women's clothes."

"How does he manage to do that and avoid women at the same time?"

Katherine was aware of the theory that hairdressers and clothes designers are misogynists, more or less to a man, and use their skills to make women look ridiculous. Who has not felt revulsion at the first sight of a new style of dress or hair only to find it *très chic* within weeks of its introduction? That designers were up to a lucrative mockery of their clientele was not inconceivable. But once more this required a deeper personality than Katherine was willing to grant Alan Derecho.

"When was the last time you saw him, Katherine?"

"When Marilyn died."

"That's a long time ago."

"Perhaps."

"I wonder what he's become in the meanwhile?"

Emtee Dempsey would not, of course, simply order Katherine to check out Alan Derecho, but it was useless to ignore such oblique suggestions. The old nun would return to the matter again and again until her will was done.

And so it was that Katherine Senski swept into Les Poupées an hour later. Clerks and customers turned to stare, astonished.

If there is a polar opposite of chic, Katherine was it, and it gave her pleasure to bewilder the denizens of Les Poupées with her unclassifiable style. What would they make of Mildred Scott in her beret and cloak and velvet jumpsuit? The offices, she guessed, would be at the end of the narrow corridor at the back of the store. And sure enough, MONSIEUR ALAN was inscribed on the door at the end of the corridor. Katherine knocked, but the door was not tightly shut and swung open.

●

The man behind the desk used both hands to hold the gun he trained on Katherine.

THREE 3

BENJAMIN RUSH MET the legal representatives of the Archdiocese of Chicago and those of the Moran family in a conference room of his firm's offices high in the Sears Tower. Monsignor Lipski, a member of the entourage of the cardinal, was there with Clavell. Butler represented Swift, Swallow, Finch, and Robinson. Lipski marveled at the view and cocked an eye at Benjamin Rush.

"Will you tempt me with the offer that I shall be master of all I survey?"

"I know you would refuse." Rush hoped his smile was diplomatic. He did not like flippant scriptural references, least of all from the clergy.

Monsignor Lipski's voice lowered. "You mustn't think the cardinal really shares the belief that Sister Mary Teresa spirited the young nun away."

"I doubt that these lawyers really believe that either."

But it was difficult to think so during the hour that followed. Clavell, speaking for the Moran family, said that his clients would be satisfied simply to be told the whereabouts of Donna Moran.

"As you know, pretrial depositions have yet to be taken." A look of remembered frustration traveled across the expanse of Clavell's forehead. He had cooled his heels in the Carmelite parlor in Missouri to no purpose. He had been refused an opportunity to speak with Donna Moran, even through the grille, and had returned to Chicago seething with anger. He would have initiated a suit against the convent, claiming they were keeping Donna Moran there against her will, but Randy Moran had vetoed that. He knew better.

"Sister Mary Magdalene has been kidnapped," Benjamin Rush replied. "Your energies would be better spent seeking to find her."

"That is why we're here, Benjamin," Clavell said. He held an unlit cigar as a token of his power of will. Once he had smoked a minimum of eight cigars a day. Now he carried one about unlit, tossing it out at the end of the day. "She was allegedly kidnapped from the home of your client."

Butler chimed in. "Who smuggled her into the city, or tried to. When that didn't work, when she was discovered, the kidnapping was staged."

"Sister Mary Teresa promised the young nun's superior that she would be safe in Chicago. That was the reason for her unannounced arrival."

"Unannounced!"

"Sister Mary Teresa is abject that her ward was taken from the house while the rest of the nuns were at Holy Name Cathedral for morning Mass."

The sides were clearly defined from the outset. Though the cardinal's attorneys disliked being in tandem with the Moran lawyer, they were of one mind that the kidnapping was part of the same plan that had involved the hiring of Mildred Scott to mislead the press at O'Hare. Rush's retort that it was Mildred Scott's desire to get personal publicity out of the plan that explained the press being there when the flight from St. Louis came in was met with scorn.

Rush stood his ground, of course, responding icily to any

and all suggestions that his client could conceivably be guilty of the staged kidnapping that his opponents firmly believed had taken place. It did not help that Rush had to repress memories of the times in the past when Emtee Dempsey had engaged in deception, indeed had deceived even himself. But he steadfastly refused to acknowledge the plausibility of the charges being made. That there seemed to be no vigorous pursuit of the alleged kidnappers was difficult to deny, but that of course was something they should take up with the police.

"Has any ransom been demanded?"

"Perhaps that question should be put to the Morans."

"What has Sister Mary Teresa done if she is so abject?"

"We are offering a reward for information leading to the arrest and conviction of the kidnappers."

"This is the first I've heard of it." Clavell brought his cigar to his mouth.

"Fifty thousand dollars."

Benjamin Rush acted on his own authority in announcing this reward, but then if it came to that, it was he who would have to pay it. Undeniably, in coming up with the reward to stave off a line of questioning, he had the sense that he was engaged in a make-believe effort. The man facing him across the oak table would never have guessed that Benjamin Rush, in his heart of hearts, thought that the disappearance of Sister Mary Magdalene had indeed been engineered by Emtee Dempsey.

The main result of that meeting for himself was the conviction that the other lawyers presented their case quite sincerely. He had hoped to surprise some lack of earnestness on their part, some slight clue that would suggest that this complaint was a ruse to disguise the fact that they knew where Donna Moran was. The most plausible kidnapper was her brother, but if he had indeed done it, his lawyer was unaware of it.

94

Sister Mary Teresa nodded when he conveyed to her his conviction that neither of the other two interested parties knew the whereabouts of Donna Moran.

"No, I don't suppose I really thought they did. One might imagine a Cardinal Richelieu employing a little private habeas corpus, but no more, no more." She sounded almost sad. "As for Randolph Moran, that's another matter. You're convinced in their case as well?"

"Sister, the most evident fact of the meeting was that they were both certain that *we* are concealing Sister Mary Magdalene."

"Oh, dear God, how I wish that were true."

His skepticism was almost totally overcome by this clearly heartfelt remark, but over the years he had come to know that, without technically dissembling, Emtee Dempsey had a repertoire of nuanced moral stances that would dazzle the most adroit canon lawyer. He knew that she could be sincerely expressing her wish that the young Carmelite were with her there on Walton Street while at the same time knowing that she was safely stashed in, say, the lake house in Indiana that had been, in Sister Mary Teresa's phrase, one of the few fragments shored against her ruin when her sisters in religion succumbed to the wiles of the world and turned in their veils for a more ordinary kind of life. Benjamin Rush made a mental note to have someone check out the lake house, discreetly. Further than that he did not choose to go. He most certainly would not put the old nun directly to the question. Direct questions posed no threat to her if she chose to conceal something. Double effect, mental reservation, some wrinkle in the definition of lying, would enable her to do what the uninstructed might regard as intentionally deceiving him. That one ought never to lie was a moral absolute; she could become poetic in its defense. But everything lay in the deed that was to be accounted a lie. It was not that Rush feared leading the old nun into temptation with a direct question about the whereabouts of Sister Mary Magdalene. Rather he did not wish to put her ingenuity to the test and put himself in the position of a lawyer who was his client's fool.

"Have the police no leads on where she is, Sister?"

"If they do they are keeping it from me. Would they be so cruel?"

Richard Moriarity would not regard it as cruelty to keep from his old nemesis whatever leads the police had come upon. The lawyer called downtown from Emtee Dempsey's study, but Moriarity was not in his office. Rush put the phone down and looked across the room at a bookshelf where a uniform set of the Fathers of the Church glistened in red and gold. Was there a set of the Mothers of the Church?

"What bothers me, Sister, is that no one seems to be treating this as a kidnapping. Those with whom I just met think we are playing games with them. We in turn suspected that one of them would know where Donna Moran is. I doubt that the police are taking it more seriously than the rest of us."

"The rest of us? I assure you, Benjamin, that the disappearance of that young nun from this house weighs most heavily on my heart. I assured her superior that here she would be safe. Leaving her alone while we went to Mass was, in retrospect, a very stupid thing to do. I would give a week in heaven to have that decision to make over again." She lifted her eyes as if to seal the bargain. "But you are right, Benjamin. We alone know what happened. The burden accordingly devolves on us. I shall proceed as if in effect deputized to do the work of the police."

"And what will you do?"

She looked at him for a moment. "Am I correct in thinking that you are a director of Midstate Paper?"

"How on earth did you know that?"

"Then it's true?"

"It is."

She sighed. "That is where we must begin. There is something I want you to do for me."

And, as he drew his chair closer to the desk, all Benjamin Rush's doubts about the old nun's sincerity left him. Together they would accomplish what the police seemed insufficiently inspired to do.

R ANDY MORAN WAS not a reading man, but he was well
enough informed on the lives of Henry Ford, John D.
Rockefeller, Andrew Carnegie and other successful men
to have attained a vantage point on his father's reputation
that provided some consolation. Not much, but some. It was
clear that the successful are pursued by schools of pilot fish
whose main purpose in the larger scheme is to feast off the
achievements of the great by trying to prove that they were not
only no better than the average man but a helluva lot worse.

This information had come his way through digests and
summaries of the relevant biographies. In school Randy had
paid the price for such success as he had known—buying
tutorial help as well as previous exams in the courses he was
taking, buying term papers. He had actually won a prize for a
term paper in business ethics in which the ethics of buying
term papers was the theme. The author had demanded a bonus
for this unlooked-for result but thought better of it when Randy
threatened to expose his thriving business.

The reaction of the archdiocese to the gift of a million of
Moran money had threatened the foundation of Randy's view

of life. His philosophy was, in its essentials, that the money his father had amassed was sufficient wherewithal to obtain anything worth having. He had reached a point in his life when he found it intolerable that the family of a man as powerful and prominent as his father should be looked down upon by those whose ethics were identical with his late father's or, and this was the subclass he found most odious, were several saving generations removed from the pirates whose fortunes they enjoyed. Résumés of the lives of the great robber barons, automobile, railroad and steel magnates, suggested the solution. Philanthropy.

Giving a million to the Archdiocese of Chicago should have been a stone that got more than one bird, both church and state, so to speak. The cardinal's reaction had stirred Randy's wrath as nothing had before. He was in a situation analogous to that of a woman scorned. And, needless to say, a good part of his reaction was because of a woman. He had conceived the notion of making Sylvia Fogarty his wife, and the ties of the Fogartys with the Catholic Church in Chicago had determined the direction of his own essays in philanthropy, but the gesture meant to erase from the Fogarty mind memories of past Moran peccadilloes had the effect of stirring up once more all the unsubstantiated charges against Ignatius Moran. Those who had feared him alive were now untroubled by worries as to what Iggie might do in retaliation. Well, they had reckoned without the wrath of Randy Moran.

His immediate purpose was to get back the gift from the archdiocese along with a sizable amount for defamation of character. He had not smiled upon Clavell's proposal that they combine forces with the cardinal's lawyers to pry Donna from the hiding spot to which the nuns on Walton Street had moved her. His feelings about his sister the Carmelite were mixed.

On the one hand, it turned out that Sylvia and her family were visibly moved by the reminder that one of Iggie Moran's daughters had given her life to God in an austere convent in Missouri. On the other hand, Donna's unwillingness to come to the aid of her father's reputation had introduced the possibility of a schism among the Morans which, at the present moment, could prove fatal. It was a possibility he had never even imagined.

Randy's own relation to the faith of his fathers—or at least of his mother—was clouded. In the parlance of a local sociologist, he qualified as an Ethnic Catholic, meaning he was a Catholic in somewhat the same sense that he was a Chicagoan. He was aware of his father's return to religious practice. Perhaps someday, when Sylvia became his wife, he too would mend his ways. At the moment even acknowledging the existence of the deity seemed a concession to his enemies. After all, Donna spent her life in prayer. He scowled, remembering the remark in the *Trib* that Donna had withdrawn to Missouri to do penance for the whole family.

Lenore and Joe presented no worry. Cremona had pursued Donna until she entered the convent and then had turned to Lenore. One would have been naive not to suspect such persistence. Cremona seemed determined to link himself to the Moran family one way or the other. Only that turned out not to be it. He settled down in Oak Park and went on working for Midstate Paper, and the two times Randy had suggested to his brother-in-law that there could be more lucrative kinds of employment he had drawn a blank. He concluded that Cremona was simply not too bright. Which made him a good match for Lenore. Donna would have been beyond Joe even if she hadn't become a Carmelite.

Wiley's resurrection of the Marilyn Derecho affair made it mandatory that Donna come to the defense of her father and her old friend. Randy had known of his father's fixation with Marilyn, though it was unclear whether it had gone beyond a harmless sugar daddy thing. In any case, no matter what was leaked from the prosecutor's office, there was no way Wiley could establish the connection. If Iggie Moran had paid Marilyn's way through law school, it could not be traced. If he had paid the rent on the apartment in which she lived, his largess had been so indirect no one could have traced it in his lifetime. But what could be more decisive to silence the innuendoes than the deposition of a Carmelite nun that such accusations against her father and Marilyn were slanderous?

Clavell had been unable to speak with Donna when he flew to Missouri for that purpose. Randy telephoned and had never in his life received so decisive a refusal delivered in such mild tones. He flew to Missouri himself and pleaded with the extern sister to let him speak with Donna.

"This is a cloistered convent, Mr. Moran. The nuns receive visitors only in the most extraordinary circumstances."

"This is extraordinary."

"Sister Mary Magdalene thinks not."

"I'm diabetic," he said, irrationally. "She knows that. Let me talk to her."

"This is a cloistered convent, Mr. Moran."

It was like a recorded message. Randy looked desperately at the grille behind which Donna lived, out of his reach. He went to Mass in the church, but the nuns were separated from the congregation by a grille that slid open when Mass began. He could see vaguely silhouetted through the grille the figures of nuns. He could not see Donna but she could see him. If she chose to notice. He might have faked a diabetic coma, but by this time he believed that she would not allow herself to be distracted by those who attended Mass on the worldly side of the grille.

It was Wiley's subpoena that broke the ice, and it pained Randy to think that the prosecutor had been able to do what he could not. Of course he had been as surprised as anyone to learn that the Carmelites had finally decided that Donna should return to Chicago. The fiasco at O'Hare when the press had been deceived by Mildred Scott, the actress's revelation of her employer and the consequent descent upon Walton Street with the claim that Donna had been mysteriously kidnapped while the nuns were off at the cathedral for morning Mass, was just the kind of media attention Randy had dreaded. The only question was where the hell had they stashed Donna?

His lawyer returned from the conference in Benjamin Rush's office convinced that Rush did not know where Sister Mary Magdalene was.

"The cardinal?"

Clavell shook his head. "His people wouldn't have wasted all that time just to deceive us."

"But those nuns would."

"Maybe. But not Benjamin Rush."

The trouble with lawyers was that you had to trust them. Up to a point. Like Iggie before him, Randy employed different lawyers for different tasks. Confidentiality was not what it seemed if any disgruntled counselor who decided that what he had learned in confidence was illegal was thereby absolved of any obligation to shut up about it. By and large, lawyers were such con men that Randy considered it likely that they were particularly vulnerable to the schemes of one another. And he knew Benjamin Rush sufficiently well to know that he was in another class than Clavell and anyone on the cardinal's team.

Of course even Rush could be deceived by that old nun on Walton Street.

"Did Rush know about the hiring of Mildred Scott?"

Clavell thought about it. He didn't know. If Sister Mary Teresa Dempsey had kept her lawyer in the dark about the O'Hare episode, she could do the same with the fake kidnapping. By not telling him, she protected him. Randy felt a lot more affinity with the old nun than with anyone else in this whole business. That was an odd thought, but it was by putting himself in her shoes that Randy had his great idea.

He shagged Clavell out of the room so he could enjoy the realization to the fullest. Standing at his window, he grinned out over Chicago like some latter-day gargoyle. His window looked south, toward Missouri, toward the convent where he could now believe Donna continued to live her cloistered life at this very minute.

After all, who had seen her? The commotion at the airport involved a publicity-hungry actress employed, she said, to mislead the press so that Donna could get safely into town without being bothered by reporters. Then, the story went, Mildred Scott, unwilling to have brought off a triumph of acting that would be known only to herself, the nuns on Walton Street and God, had announced that Donna was with Sister Mary Teresa Dempsey. The media descended on the house only to be told that the Carmelite had been kidnapped. Randy grinned and shook his head in grudging admiration. All these events were perfectly compatible with the supposition that Donna had never left her convent in Missouri.

His smile began to dim, as doubts about his idea formed. Had Donna been booked on that flight from St. Louis or not? But surely they would have thought of that. If she had been, there was no reason to take Mildred Scott at her word. The actress might have flown in from St. Louis under Donna's name. The real question was a simple one. Had anyone at all laid eyes on Donna since she supposedly came to Chicago? Anyone other than those involved in the deception, that is.

Randy realized that he should have thought of some such device himself to remove Donna from the prosecutor's effort to subpoena her and force her presence at the trial. He regretted now having listened to Clavell and letting him join forces with the cardinal's lawyers against Benjamin Rush. Sister Mary Teresa had done his work for him, if his guess was right. He had half a mind to drive over there and let her know he'd figured it out. He did not anticipate the same reception on Walton Street that he had received at the Carmelite convent in Missouri.

But at that point Sylvia Fogarty phoned from Sarasota.

"Randy, how awful for you, I just heard about it and I can't believe anyone would commit the sacrilege of actually kidnapping a sister. Is there any news?"

Seldom had her voice been so full of gentleness and concern when talking to him. Here was an unlooked-for bonus of the events of the past few days, events on which he had just gained a wholly new perspective.

"It's more difficult for mother, of course. She can't keep from imagining the worst."

"Oh, they wouldn't!"

"Anyone who would kidnap a nun would stop at nothing, Sylvia."

"Oh, the poor thing. And your mother. My heart goes out to her."

"The libelous attacks on my father's memory are bad enough, but Donna has been the apple of her eye since she entered the convent."

"Randy, is there anything I can do?"

His eyes glazed. "Just hearing from you means everything, Sylvia."

THE HANDS HOLDING the gun trembled and Katherine realized the man behind the desk was at least as terrified as she was. But his fear gave way to embarrassment and he lowered the gun.

"Who the hell are you?"

"Who were you expecting?"

"What do you mean, busting in here like that? I might have shot you."

"Why?"

He lifted the gun again. "Get out of here!"

"You should remember me, Alan. Katherine Senski of the *Tribune*"

"Get out!"

He leapt to his feet, his face distorted, the gun bobbing nervously in his hand. Katherine got out of there. On her way through the store, one of the salespersons turned and gave her a meaningless smile.

"There's a madman back there," Katherine said.

"I know!" The mannequin smile did not waver. Katherine felt that she had unwittingly told a joke.

Outside, she breathed deeply as someone released from prison after a long term might breathe the air of freedom. She stood on the loading ramp of the remodeled warehouse and looked at the window of the boutique. Les Poupées. F. X. Nicolo Creations. Alan Derecho was right, he might have shot her. The man was so keyed up he could have pulled the trigger without really meaning to. If he was that frightened, why did he sit in his office waiting for the enemy to come? Someone from the Morans, no doubt. Beware a cornered coward.

This was a considered judgment. When Marilyn Derecho was found dead and Katherine was sure that, finally, Iggie Moran could be brought down, she had gone to Alan in the expectation that Marilyn's family would join in a campaign to bring Iggie to justice. The parents had been too bewildered but refused to say anything, in private or public, that could be construed as linking their dead daughter to Iggie Moran. Alan had undermined that by his futile attempt to run down Iggie Moran from which he had emerged as a bogus hero. Katherine was no more successful at the condominium where Marilyn had lived and where she had died. Her neighbors claimed to be the most incurious in the world, never having seen anyone at all, let alone Iggie Moran, come to Marilyn Derecho's apartment.

"Did you ever see her?" Katherine demanded of the manager. His name was Horace, and he had the face of a potato.

"Hey, I work for these people, I don't spy on them."

Thus had gone aglimmering the last best chance to bring Iggie Moran's career to a fitting end. It served Alan Derecho right that he should now sit cowering in his office, threatening visitors with a gun he very likely had never used.

Five minutes after leaving Alan Derecho's office, Katherine began to tremble in delayed recognition of the risk she had run. Imagine being gunned down in a glitzy boutique on the North Side. Experience told her how statistically unlikely it is that anyone dies with dramatic fittingness, the end writing an appropriate *finis* to the life. Nonetheless she prayed that God would not abandon her in her old age but bring her safely and with dignity home. Such thoughts predictably directed her to the door of her old friend, ally and mentor.

Joyce answered the door and stepped back to let Katherine in. "They just went onto the sun porch."

"They?"

The sound of a television was audible and Katherine found Emtee Dempsey and Kim sitting forward, staring at the screen while Linda Pastorini operated the remote control. Emtee Dempsey made an 180-degree turn in order to see Katherine, and beckoned her to have a chair.

"You'll be interested in this."

"This" had to do with the videotape the Cable News reporter was showing on the VCR, her interview with B.G. Briggs at O'Hare three nights ago. Katherine sat, feeling slightly peeved at being upstaged by a television reporter, and since she was expected to watch Linda at work, interviewing the hapless women's garment salesman from St. Louis, her frown deepened.

"Not a clear picture," Emtee Dempsey observed, when Linda froze the film. A wavering line bisected the screen and a quivering Linda had just turned from Briggs toward the camera.

"Just over Briggs's right shoulder."

"Oh, I see him, dear. But not clearly."

"Georgie is developing stills. They'll be much clearer. Now look at this."

She fast forwarded, then let the tape run at normal speed. Nonetheless, it was a vertiginous experience because the picture bounced around, showing a floor, then lifted, turned down again, showed a doorway and then outside and here the picture firmed.

"I told him to go see if Donna Moran was still outside and he just kept his finger on the button. Here it is!"

107

The picture on the television cleared. A night scene, traffic, people waiting on the walk. The picture froze.

"It's the same man," Linda said. "I'm sure of it. Georgie's sure of it."

The tape was shown again and again, and Katherine's pique was gone when the significance of what they were seeing became clear. Linda was saying that the man in the background, the man outside on the walk, was the man who had been given directions by Briggs and had taken off after the VW in which Donna Moran had been driven here to Walton Street.

"That is Briggs he is speaking with on the walk?" Katherine asked.

For answer, Linda ran the tape back and forth from her interview to the outside scene.

"Who is he?" Emtee Dempsey asked.

"His name? I don't know. But we know what he did. He kidnapped Donna Moran."

They adjourned to the study to pursue the matter. Emtee Dempsey seemed strangely reluctant to make the logical leap Linda had.

"It goes back to the other morning. There were no signs that the door had been forced. It seems clear that Donna opened the door to someone."

"Or just walked out," Kim murmured.

"Or just walked out," Emtee Dempsey conceded. "But if she opened the door, I maintain she would only do so if she knew the one who rang."

"Wouldn't she have to open the door to find out?" Linda asked.

"No." But Emtee Dempsey left it to Kim to explain the two vantage points from which the porch could be inspected.

Even as they sat there, Georgie arrived with the stills. He remained in the doorway of the study, as if he had come to the Ladies by mistake. Finally Joyce took him away to the kitchen.

"Come, Katherine," Sister Mary Teresa said when the

photographs had been laid out on her desk. She moved her elbowed architect's lamp so that the light shone directly on the pictures. Katherine crossed the room slowly, not liking this supporting role, and leaned over the glossy photographs. She recognized him easily.

"I don't believe it!"

"Who is it?"

She closed her eyes, the name would not come. "He is the man who was lurking about outside the night Donna arrived. He's married to the other Moran daughter."

"Joseph Cremona?"

"Yes!"

And Emtee Dempsey looked up at her as if she had just said the brightest thing in the world.

"Thank you, Katherine. And thank you, Linda. I am going to ask you all to stay. I am expecting Benjamin Rush, and my hope is that he will have something further to tell us about Mr. Joseph Cremona."

A N HOUR LATER Mr. Rush had not returned and Emtee Dempsey, visibly making the best of it, announced that the lawyer must not be coming after all.

"In the meantime, Linda, I suggest that these photographs be turned over to the police."

"I tried to reach Richard Moriarity."

"Well, let's try again." Emtee Dempsey nodded at the phone and Kim picked it up and dialed the familiar number. Why did she hope that she too would be unable to reach Richard? It was silly to think she detected a submerged coquetry in Linda's remark about trying to reach her brother, her happily married brother. Just because the woman had been married several times and had made a date with B. G. Briggs, a man she scarcely knew, did not make her a Jezebel. It was better to think of Linda as a woman who, through no fault of her own, had picked a number of lemons in the garden of love. She had picked another in Briggs, who turned out to have a wife in St. Louis. Had Linda even cared that Briggs was married? Of course it was Richard who was Kim's real concern. Men were so weak when it came to temptations of the flesh. Emtee Dempsey had a hilarious set piece lecture in which she enumerated the turns in world history that were explained because of some man's illicit lust for a woman. Somehow the old nun managed to put the burden of blame on the man. How could a woman fail to be attractive, after all, men being what they are?

Richard was in.

"Linda Pastorini and her photographer have pictures of the man they believe kidnapped Sister Mary Magdalene."

"Ah, the phantom kidnapper."

"Katherine Senski identifies him as Joseph Cremona. He is married—"

"To Iggie's other daughter. Are you serious?"

"Linda wants to turn the pictures over to you."

"Where is she?"

"Right here."

Kim handed the phone to Linda. Emtee Dempsey made a gesture and Kim leaned over so that the old nun could whisper in her ear.

"Sister Kimberly, I want you to go to Oak Park as fast as you can. Lenore has some terrible times ahead of her and she will need support."

The thought of making that long drive to Oak Park in the afternoon traffic filled Kim with gloom, and for a moment it occurred to her that the old nun's good-heartedness would be more impressive if it did not always fall to others to execute her benevolent intentions. But then she thought of Lenore and knew that she'd want to go even if Emtee Dempsey had not suggested it. In some way Kim did not understand, Joe Cremona was mixed up in what had happened to Lenore's sister. Kim almost feared Joyce would be sent along. Now she wanted that long drive as an opportunity to consider the meaning of the bewildering events of the past several days.

Behind the wheel of the VW, Kim could almost see Sister Mary Magdalene there in the passenger seat beside her as they had driven from O'Hare. What a feeling of triumph she and

111

Joyce had then, everything was working so perfectly. That Mildred Scott had done her work well was clear from the fact that their Carmelite guest had made it downstairs to 'the baggage carousel unaccompanied by the press. Of course they hadn't known then how Mildred had ensured that there would be journalists to deceive when the plane from St. Louis pulled up to the gate. Sister's bag was among the first to tumble onto the carousel, and they were out of the terminal and across the street to the short-term parking in less than ten minutes. It was a bit deflating that Sister Mary Magdalene seemed to have no sense of the adventure she was caught up in. At the time, Kim had felt chastened by her otherworldly indifference. Ah, that she and Joyce could practice such indifference to the fleeting events of this vale of tears.

It was the vulnerability of the young nun that had made her disappearance more horrible, and Emtee Dempsey's conjecture that Donna must have opened the door to someone seemed like whistling in the dark. It was too awful to think that the young Carmelite had fallen into the hands of some . . . some sexual creep. None of them mentioned that, of course. It was less upsetting to see the disappearance as connected with the reason for the Carmelite's coming to Chicago in the first place, but there was no overlooking the fact that the neighborhood around the house on Walton Street was not what it had been when Frank Lloyd Wright's plan had been executed there. Not that it was simply a matter of neighborhood. Violence was done to women and children everywhere nowadays. Why was it that sex, the symbol of love, should be the basis for so much violence in the world?

But as the days passed another thought had come. The easiest explanation of Sister Mary Magdalene's absence was that she had simply left. True, she had wanted to come to the cathedral with them that morning, but perhaps she had hoped to slip away then. Slip away where? Nothing more sinister than a desire to talk to her brother, to do what she could to complete the reason for her visit and go home to her convent. What then?

Kim shook her head violently to rid it of these thoughts. It made no sense to be telling herself imaginary stories about what might have happened. Those photographs of Linda Pastorini and the identification of the man in them as Joseph Cremona gave new significance to Lenore's remark that Joe had been in love with both sisters, that he had become her husband largely because Donna had decided to become a nun. The pictures of Joe lurking about O'Hare when the plane from St. Louis came in suggested that his interest in the other sister had not ceased.

The traffic was even worse than she had feared but had the happy effect of interrupting her thinking. Earlier, unable to devote an unbroken period of time to what had happened, she had imagined that she longed to do that. Now she knew that she did not. It was far more important that she get to Lenore and provide what buffer she could against what might be in store for the poor woman.

When she pulled into the driveway of the Cremona house in Oak Park there were two cars already parked in it. Still, there was more than enough room for the VW. She got out and started toward the house but stopped to look at the Lincoln Town Car in the drive. Just like Mr. Rush's. Ahead of it was a Jeep. The door of the house opened and Mr. Rush looked out at her.

"Are you alone, Sister?"

Kim went on to the door. "Just me."

"Sister, don't come in, stay back . . ."

Abruptly, Mr. Rush was pulled out of the doorway and was replaced by a younger man.

"C'mon," he said, making brisk movements with his hand. Kim recognized him as the man in Georgie's stills rather than the husband who had come to the house on Walton Street to pick up his wife and kids. Joseph Cremona. This realization kept her moving dreamlike toward the door and his out-

113

stretched hand. He grasped her wrist and pulled her inside, where she stood feeling like an idiot. Mr. Rush had fallen back onto a couch and was trying to regain his balance. Lenore, white faced, her children about her, looked caught up in a dream.

"He kidnapped Sister Mary Magdalene," Mr. Rush said with calm dignity, now that he was seated upright.

"Donna Moran! Her name is Donna. Sister Mary Magdalene no longer exists."

"What have you done with her, Joe?" Lenore spoke with eerie calmness.

Her husband wheeled on her, his face working, but no words emerged. He made an angry gesture and stalked across the room. His eyes were wild as he said in a choked voice, "This isn't the way I planned it."

Kim went to Lenore and took Julia in her arms. It was bad enough that this was happening but infinitely worse to be a witness to Lenore's humiliation. Her husband had begun to babble, pleading his own cause.

"She talks about what God wants. I know what God wants. It's what he always wanted. She was wrong to go away and leave me . . . ."

Lenore listened expressionlessly as her husband said in effect that he had never loved her, that these years of marriage really didn't count, not with God, God wanted him and Donna to be together. "She is my wife, really. God means people for one another."

Lenore hugged the baby closer and shut her eyes, pressing tears from them that ran down her face. She was being told that in the divine scheme as her husband understood it, she and her children did not exist, they were simply a ploy to bring home to Donna what a mistake she had made by entering the convent and leaving him. Well, he had showed her. He married her sister. He had children. That showed her. She could become a nun and he could marry Lenore but that didn't change anything.

114

"What have you done with her?" Mr. Rush asked.

A sly look came over Cremona's face. "She won't be found."

"Have you killed her?"

"Killed her?" The question shocked Cremona. "Are you crazy? After all these years, do you think . . ." A strangled derisive laugh.

"Where is she, Joe?" Lenore did not look at him or open her eyes when she asked this.

He ignored her. Rush said, "He asked me to follow him. He said he would take me to her. The phone on Walton Street was busy the one time I managed to dial it."

Gallant old Mr. Rush with his patrician manner and unfailing devotion to Sister Mary Teresa. She had asked him to ask Joe what he had done with Sister Mary Magdalene. Clearly the old nun had picked up the significance of Lenore's remark that her husband would not have married her if Donna hadn't entered the convent. How untroubled an admission that had been but could never be again. Joe had offered to take Mr. Rush to Donna and instead had led him to his home in Oak Park. Why?

"I have to think!" Cremona had followed Kim's conversation with Mr. Rush. He began to walk back and forth in the room. His wife and children seemed not to exist for him. Julia followed her father with her eyes, but he ignored her, a picture of a man trying unsuccessfully to think, trying to imagine some way out of the crazy situation in which he had involved himself. He had destroyed his wife's love with careless cutting words, but that bothered him not at all. He wanted to hit upon some scheme that would enable him to disappear with Donna Moran. Kim no longer feared that Cremona had harmed the nun. That was the only bright spot in this otherwise bleak encounter.

Lenore handed the baby to Kim and got up and started out of the room.

"Where are you going?"

Joe grabbed her arm, but she shook herself free and was gone. He turned, looked at Rush and then at Kim, decided he must keep watch on them.

"Tell us where Donna is," Kim said.

"Are you kidding?"

"Surely you don't think you can just carry her off against her will. She is a nun now, it doesn't matter what your feelings for her were."

"Shut up!"

"What you must do, Joe," Mr. Rush said, his voice confiding, "is take me to Sister Mary Magdalene. You have done a foolish thing. Don't compound your folly."

He stopped. His eyes went to Lenore, who stood in the kitchen doorway, a rifle in hand, no longer the obsequious spouse. Lenore Moran was manifestly her father's daughter. She raised the rifle and pointed it at her husband.

"Where is Donna?"

He studied her and the weapon for a moment, like a child confronting a problem in mathematics. Then he solved it. "That's your BB gun." A smile formed on his lips and he looked at Rush, to share this intelligence. "She scares away raccoons with it."

There was a *pftting* sound and Cremona cried out. His hand went to his upper arm. Lenore cocked the gun and once more trained it on her husband.

"Tell us where Donna is?"

His expression fluctuated between fear and disbelief that she thought she could threaten him with a BB gun. Again there was a *pffft* and he yelped in pain, scuttling away from her, into a corner of the room. Lenore cocked the rifle and then did so again and again, increasing the air pressure in the rifle's chamber.

"Goddam it, Lenore, cut that out."

She shot him again, the pellet embedding itself in the flesh of his arm. He looked with horror at the shiny copper around which blood began to ooze. Meanwhile, Benjamin Rush was on the phone.

Kim took the children out of the room now that it was clear that Lenore had her husband at bay and was not at all reluctant to keep shooting him with the air gun until he agreed to take Mr. Rush to where he was keeping Sister Mary Magdalene. It didn't seem right to Kim that she herself should take such satisfaction from seeing a man who had inflicted such terrible pain on his wife be repaid with physical pain and the humiliation of having it administered by Lenore and with such an absurd weapon.

Perhaps Joseph Cremona was as relieved as Kim when the squad cars pulled up at the curb and uniformed members of the Oak Park police came loping across the lawn to the door.

SEVEN

SHE AND GEORGIE took a cab, not wanting to run the risk that any of the competition would notice the Cable News van and cheat them of exclusive coverage of the rescue of Donna Moran, the young Carmelite who had been kidnapped shortly after returning to Chicago to testify in the posthumous investigation of her father's role in the death of her friend Marilyn Derecho. It was damned nice of Emtee Dempsey, as they called her, to play it straight and let her in on the big finale, given the fact that Georgie's pictures of her interview with Briggs had proved to be the Open Sesame seed. Not everyone would have recognized an obligation.

As for herself, apart from the professional satisfaction of heading for an exclusive, there was the sense that she was somehow vindicating the death of poor old Briggs. The bastard had been married after all, not that they had discussed the subject, but did you have to discover a man was a husband before he had to act like one? But what had he actually done? Sure, she had recognized the expectation in his eyes at O'Hare. After she said she'd meet him at the Palmer House, she herself had done a little speculating along the same lines, but they hadn't done anything. Nothing could change that. After she saw the stern gruff-voiced wife on a video sent up from St. Louis, Linda didn't blame Briggs for wanting a little change. What turns women into such forbidding bitches? Marriage, she wanted to say, only she didn't believe it. It wasn't marriage, it was the people you married that ruined everything.

Beside her, Georgie whistled through his teeth and played his fingers nervously on the steering wheel. Forty years old going on seventeen, Georgie got into more trouble, psychic and physical, than Linda herself had ever known. There were still the remains of his puzzlement when she gave him the address Emtec Dempsey read over the phone.

"Does that mean anything to you?" the old nun asked.

"I was about to ask you the same thing."

"It's near where our college was."

Which meant nothing to Linda. Nor to Georgie, who frowned, as if inspecting a mental map of Chicago and environs.

There was nothing discreet about the way the police clogged the street with cars, double-parked so that George had a time squeezing the van between them.

"Geez," Georgie said, interrupting his sibilant whistling.

"At least they waited for us. Know where we are?"

"Tell me."

"This is where Marilyn Derecho lived."

Georgie decided to double-park himself. "Think he's giving us the runaround?"

"Well, we're not alone."

They owed it to Joe Cremona, it turned out, that the police had waited. He would make no move until the press was there to cover the event. But he looked disappointed as Linda and Georgie came up.

"Where are the others?"

"We're the pool."

He thought about it, decided that was acceptable, or maybe

119

he didn't understand. In any case, it was a lie. Not that the competition wouldn't be using their coverage, for a fee. Richard Moriarity clearly didn't like the suggestion that Cremona was in charge of this event. He grabbed him by an arm, causing him to cry out.

"Take it easy, I've been shot."

Gleason and O'Connell, two assistants of Moriarity, took up stations on either side of Cremona. Moriarity glared at him. He addressed the camera.

"I brought Donna here several days ago, for safekeeping. I told her there was something I wanted to show her at Marilyn's apartment. She was reluctant to come, but I said it was important to help her father."

"How so?"

Cremona looked at Linda. "I said it to get her to come with me."

"You mean you lied to her."

"Love is exempted from rules of that kind. I meant her well. I love her. That is what is important."

Important to whom? It was tempting to want to argue with him. But what was the point, he was a nut, locking up a nun in an apartment where her best friend had died. In the elevator on the way up, he babbled on, and Georgie kept the camera on him. Maybe that's why he kept babbling. This was the high point of his life, an historic event: Joseph Cremona, a fool for love, reveals hiding place of kidnapped nun.

On the eleventh floor the doors slid open. As if in a mirror, the elevator across from theirs opened and Gleason and O'Connell and some uniformed police stepped out, the event recorded by Georgie. They would have enough footage to make a movie out of this.

Cremona posed at a door, the key in his hand, about to unlock the apartment. Moriarity groaned until the camera swung to him and then he beetled his brows and looked in charge. What would that poor nun think when this menagerie burst in on her?

Cremona turned the key in the dead bolt lock, opened the door and entered, Georgie went next, camera whirring, then Moriarity and Linda.

"Donna," Cremona called as he preceded them. "Donna?"

The living room was white and black. White walls, white carpet, black leather furniture, glass top tables, long-necked lamps. The pictures on the wall were abstract. The room was empty. There was no answer to Cremona's plaintive calling for Donna. He turned and looked into the camera, a confused man. He seemed to debate whether he wanted to lead this parade through the rest of the apartment.

"Where's her bedroom?" Moriarity asked, and Cremona bristled at the suggestiveness of the question.

But Gleason and O'Connell had already checked the bedrooms. Nothing.

"The bathroom," Gleason said. "The door's shut."

"Locked?"

Gleason seemed unsure what to make of the implication that he would have broken in on the Carmelite when she was in the bathroom. Moriarity looked at Linda and she nodded. Georgie, bless him, was right on her heels as she went down the hall to knock on the closed door of the bathroom.

No answer.

Linda put her ear against the door. "Sister?"

Her hand was on the knob now and she turned it. The door pushed inward. Linda opened it several inches and called in.

"Sister Mary Magdalene?"

Then she pushed the door all the way open and stepped inside. She came immediately to a halt. In the moment before Georgie pushed past her, Linda looked down into the sunken tub full of water in which half submerged, her clothing billowing in the water, the lifeless body of Donna Moran floated.

FOUR

THE DEATH BY drowning of Sister Mary Magdalene, OCD, in the bathtub of what had once been the apartment of her college friend Marilyn Derecho, an apartment allegedly provided by the dead nun's father, Iggie Moran, was not a one-day sensation in the local media. Linda Pastorini's scoop, her voice-over account as the vivid pictures Georgie had taken were shown, the sequence culminating in the pushing open of the bathroom door and the revelation of the dreadful scene, was shown again and again, not only on Cable News but on all the local channels and the networks as well. The camera's concentration on the clothed body submerged in the tub of water was the result of Georgie's shock when he realized what he was filming, but it had the effect of a morbid lingering on that scene of violent death with its added note of sacrilege.

"Canon law is quite clear on that," Emtee Dempsey said, as if seeking refuge from her own shock in this recherché point. "To strike let alone kill any person dedicated to God by the three vows of religion is sacrilege."

Kim was in the study when Sister Mary Teresa telephoned

the awful news to the Carmelite convent in Missouri. Their sister would never return. The journey reluctantly consented to had led to the tragic consequences that had been feared from the beginning. Of course they did not blame Emtee Dempsey. Nor did they blame themselves, as if they were in charge of the universe. Sister Mary Magdalene had been under God's protection every bit as much out of the convent as in it, and if He had chosen to take her to Himself, human wills must conform to His.

It had been difficult enough for the old nun to telephone and report the absence of Sister Mary Magdalene from the house. "The police regard it as kidnapping." Even in her consternation, Emtee Dempsey did not seek refuge behind an interpretation she did not fully share. How impossibly more difficult to call and say the young nun who had been entrusted to her care was dead, and not only dead but violently dead—murdered, drowned—and, far worse, in circumstances that called forth the prurient interests of that gang of organized gossipers called journalists.

Katherine did not demur at this description, though of course she could hardly be expected to agree. Georgie's pictures and Linda's account of the entering of the apartment in the expectation of finding a hale and hearty Donna Moran and finding instead her lifeless body had the dignified authority of an authentic event accidentally recorded. By the second day, the coverage altered in tone, shock gave way to questions, questions to innuendo, until "nun found in love nest" became synonymous with Donna Moran. It was vulgarity unleashed. Thank God the body had been found fully clothed. Thank God there had been no evidence whatsoever of sexual molestation. Quite gratuitously the pathologist observed that the deceased had been a virgin.

What Kim herself remembered most vividly was the reaction of Joseph Cremona to the finding of the corpse of Donna Moran.

He went into a state of shock. For a time he seemed to stop

breathing, as if willing himself to die so that he could be with the woman he had loved despite his marriage to her sister, despite his two children, despite the religious vows that Donna had taken. Richard deflected one of the paramedics to Joe, to make certain that he remained sufficiently in control of himself to explain what he had done.

What he claimed he had done was a repetition of the story that had brought them all to the apartment in the first place. He had taken Donna there from Walton Street.

"How did you know she was coming to Chicago?"

From the time the prosecutor and other lawyers had been seeking to bring Donna to Chicago, Joe Cremona acquainted himself with the incoming flights from St. Louis, and every day he called the airlines involved to ask if Sister Mary Magdalene Moran was on such and such a flight. Making these calls became a daily routine, and finally he had been assured that, yes, she would arrive at O'Hare that evening.

"Of course I knew the woman the press swarmed on wasn't Donna. I thought the whole thing was a fake. But I went down to baggage claim and outside where a man pointed her out in a Volkswagen. It was the other nuns that made me think of Donna's old teacher."

"So you kidnapped her?"

Cremona seemed to be speaking into an invisible tunnel, directing his words to some ear other than those of the people who preferred the distraction of Richard's interrogation to any further views of the body, then under preliminary inspection by the medical examiner.

"I lied to her."

Richard waited, but apparently Joe needed prompting. "What did you tell her?"

He tipped forward, breathed deeply, shut his eyes, grimaced. "There's something I want to show you in Marilyn's apartment, something important to clear your father."

"And she just came along with you?"

"Yes." He looked at Richard then again peered into the

127

tunnel only he could see. "She said that's why she was in Chicago, to help her father."

"How'd you get a key to this apartment?"

"From my brother-in-law."

"So you intended to bring her here."

"It was providence."

"What time was that?"

"Right after the other nuns left."

He had been parked all night in his car outside the house where at last Donna was. He had no idea what he meant to do. Only now that she was in Chicago he would not let her escape from him again.

"What happened when you got her here?"

He put his face in his hands. "I told her the truth."

Kim found it impossible not to feel sorry for the man, sitting there surrounded by people, all of them despising him for what he had done to Donna, having to speak of his passion for her in circumstances that made it seem even more absurd. The married man who had remained in love with his sister-in-law the nun. The unrequited lover who had assured Wiley that proof could be had from Donna, that Iggie Moran had set Marilyn Derecho up in this apartment. In his madness he had supposed that all he needed was to be alone with Donna and the lost years could be redeemed.

He was convinced that her life as a nun was stunted and unhappy, that once free of the routine and reminded of the real world, above all else, once confronted by his love that had only grown more powerful in her absence, she would confess she had made a mistake as grievous as his own in marrying her sister. Then they would resolve to use what was left of their lives to make amends for resisting the destiny God had decreed for them.

His stilted manner of speaking came naturally to his lips, it was not feigned to protect himself from the chill silence into which he spoke.

"What was her reaction?"

128

For the first time he seemed reluctant to speak. Expressions flickered over his face as the memories came. When he did speak, he was inaudible and Richard told him angrily to speak up.

"She wanted to go back to Walton Street."

"But you kept her here against her will?"

"I saw it would take time."

"You forced her to remain here?"

Can one who offers no resistance be forced? The Carmelite had listened to what he had to say, had told him that what he proposed was sinful, that he could not possibly just leave Lenore and the children as he proposed and that in any case she herself meant to return to her convent as quickly as possible. Obviously this trip to Chicago had been a mistake.

It was clear that Cremona heard this sensible reaction as only what might be expected from a woman who had been enclosed in a cloister for years. She needed time to adjust to the possibility that at last she could begin to live.

"I left her here to think."

"Locking her in?"

"She was used to that."

The dead bolt locks require a key to be opened from within, and she had had no key. He had also taken the precaution to remove the telephones.

"There were other ways she could have called for help."

"Help to do what?"

When the body was taken away, everyone but Richard and Joseph Cremona followed it out.

"Why did you kill her?" Richard asked.

"I didn't kill her!"

"Are you saying she committed suicide?"

He looked at Richard, shocked.

Reporting all this to Emtee Dempsey, Kim was asked to remember every detail of the scene, to describe the tone of Joseph's voice, his expressions.

"He did not react at all when her body was taken away?"

"Maybe he didn't realize what it was."

"Your account is sympathetic to him."

"He was like a captured animal."

"Do you think he killed her?"

Kim thought about it. The unreality of his manner, the preposterous scene he recounted when he had first taken Donna to that apartment, made it easy to imagine him dreamily holding her under water until there was no more life in her body.

"I don't know. He must have."

"Why?"

"Richard asked him what he intended to do when she continued to insist that she wanted to return to her convent."

"What was his answer?"

"The one he gave Katherine. Sister Mary Magdalene is no more."

2

THERE WAS NO need for Katherine to say anything when Emtee Dempsey voiced scathing things about her fellow journalists in the days following the discovery of the body of Donna Moran. Is there any profession that is immune from the criticism and even distaste of its members? Academics complain about the university, doctors about medicine, lawyers about their conscienceless colleagues, so of course a journalist could at least on occasion feel shame for her profession. Katherine Senski was not at all proud of the way the media handled the death of Sister Mary Magdalene.

Yet she did not wholly blame them for treating a woman religious as if she had been up to no good in the apartment in which her body had been found. For years the papers had been full of jogging nuns, lesbian nuns, aerobic nuns, protesting nuns, angry women who insisted that they would live their lives exactly as they pleased, no matter their vows of poverty, chastity and obedience. Obedience? The word was pronounced with a sneer.

Inevitably a nun was found who assured her interviewer that the death of Donna Moran was a direct result of the oppressive atmosphere in the kind of conservative convent in which the poor woman had been confined. No wonder that once outside in the bracing air of freedom . . .

Katherine turned it off. What incredible slander to suppose the worst about Donna Moran, despite all the evidence, and use her death as an ideological weapon.

"Sister Mary Magdalene is beyond the reach of such nonsense," Emtee Dempsey said, and it was the first time Katherine had ever detected in her old friend's voice a wistful expectation of release from this vale of tears.

"Now don't tell me you're not as anxious as I am to see that man punished for what he did."

The old nun's gaze drifted across the room. "How did he happen to have access to that apartment, Katherine?"

Cremona claimed he had been given a key to the apartment by Randy Moran, and Randy did not deny the story, though he had not been willing to discuss it with any member of the press.

But Katherine was not to be so easily deflected from discussing the fate Joseph Cremona deserved. It was like fiddling with a tooth until it ached, masochism, but Katherine could not help herself. There was a kind of mad amusement to be had from watching the old nun pretend that she had doubts about Cremona's guilt.

"I keep thinking of his wife and children."

"If he had thought of them he'd be a free man. And Donna Moran would be alive."

"Has he been arraigned?"

"This morning. First-degree murder."

"Randy Moran must have had a key to the apartment as well. He would not have given the only key to Joseph Cremona."

"Are you suggesting that Randy killed his own sister?"

"I am suggesting reason to doubt that the case against Joseph Cremona is open and shut."

"That's a legal point and you're no lawyer."

"Who is his lawyer?"

"The court will appoint one."

"I wonder if Benjamin Rush would—"

"You can't possibly mean that!"

"No, it wouldn't do. He was there when the body was found. I suppose that disqualifies him."

"Otherwise I'm sure he'd love defending the man who killed the nun kidnapped from your house."

There was an aspect of the superfluous about the arraignment and scheduled trial of Joseph Cremona. What earthly good did it do to punish him? Not that he could be allowed just to run around loose, after what he had done, but Emtee Dempsey's mention of his family touched a chord. What would Lenore do?

"I wish you'd find out, Katherine."

"Just drop in on her?"

"Oh, I'd call first."

In the end she and Sister Kimberly went together. It seemed the least they could do for Joseph Cremona's still-living victims.

Katherine was reminded of the husband being interrogated by Richard Moriarity when she sat in the living room of the house on Oak Park, with Kim beside her, holding Julia on her lap, talking to an almost catatonic Lenore Cremona. The baby was down for his nap.

"Have you seen Joe?"

"Have you, Lenore?"

"He told them to keep me away from him."

It was awful seeing a woman under the burden of such rejection. God knows it could not have been physical appearance that explained Cremona's preference for the sister. Lenore, despite her current stunned and woebegone manner, was a beautiful woman, at least as beautiful as Donna. Of course there is no explanation for physical attraction, or spiritual attraction either, for that matter. Katherine's own life had assumed the shape of a minor tragedy when she fell in love with a married man and neither of them was able to ignore that fact and obey the instinct of their hearts. It had been the only love Katherine had wanted, and when it proved impossible, she became as much of a celibate as her good friend Sister Mary Teresa. Her life had been a successful one, a satisfying one, but nonetheless lacked an emotional fullness that only married love can give. For years she had half prayed that the man would be freed by the death of his wife, a dreadful wish for which she felt guilty. In any case, like her love, it was a wish unfulfilled. He died, and it was the wife who married again, within a year, moving from happiness to happiness while Katherine continued her successful and solitary life. Lenore Cremona's plight made it clear that things could be far worse than her own situation.

Here was a beautiful woman who had gladly chosen a life of dedication to her husband and children. To all appearances their life had been happy, there was this home, the children. But surely Joe Cremona could not have completely concealed the fact that all the while his heart was elsewhere, with Donna, nurturing the impossible hope that somehow his present all-too-real life would prove a dream and he would be united with his true love. The idiot had actually expected his wife to accept his desertion of her as the will of God. After all, he was simply pursuing his destiny.

"Isn't there someone who could stay with you?"

"You mean during the funeral?"

This was not what Katherine had meant, she had been thinking of the longer run, but Lenore's response was the first indication that she planned to attend her sister's funeral. Her brother insisted that the Morans must show a united front. He obviously expected the death of his sister to write finis to the attacks on the family name. But of course the fact that the same apartment had been the scene where the woman linked with his father and now his sister had been killed, a nun who had been the doomed target of Joseph Cremona's passion, provided a peg on which all the old stories about Iggie were hung again. Nor was the spectacle of the funeral calculated to still the wagging tongues.

The wake was a social event, several thousand gawkers joining the line that went past the coffin. The coffin was closed, as the morbid discovered too late, after devoting the better part of an hour to being in line, but the atmosphere in the Chevelin Fondo Funeral Home made up for the disappoint-ment. Camped in a folding chair in a corner of the viewing room, Katherine scowled at the whispering curiosity seekers that snaked in one door and out the other. It would be nice to think they breathed an Ave for the repose of Donna Moran's soul, but it was the breath of scandal that had drawn them, the sense of being caught up in a media event. How different this public display was from the visit Sister Mary Teresa and the two younger nuns from Walton Street had paid earlier. One of the younger Chevelins had brought them into the room and then withdrawn, closing the doors behind him. Emtee Demp-sey led them in the rosary, and Katherine had the sense that she was involved in some matter-of-fact transaction with the beyond. If the old nun's faith had ever wavered, it was a secret between her and her God. She talked of such things generi-cally.

"The Little Flower had grave temptations against faith as she lay dying."

"Saint Thérèse of Lisieux?"

A nod. "She had a bleak vision of what the world and her life, all our lives, would be, if God did not exist and this brief span were all we have of existence."

"But she got over it?"

"She prayed."

The Little Flower had been a Carmelite. So too Teresa of Avila, from whom Emtee Dempsey derived her religious name.

"Did you ever think of joining the Carmelites?"

"I joined the Order of Martha and Mary."

That was part of her solidity, not to look back at crossroads and imagine what it would have been like to take another path.

The funeral Mass the following day was held in the cathedral, the celebrant one of the auxiliary bishops, the cardinal being in Rome. Katherine wondered if he had flown off on the spur of the moment to avoid any more complications with the Moran family.

The Moran family. At the moment that came down to the Widow Moran, Randy, Lenore and her two children. Lenore looked half a nun herself with the great black mantilla enfolding her head, solemn little Julia at her side. The baby was with Sister Joyce on Walton Street, just a few blocks away. Randy, following the casket of his slain sister up the main aisle, the pews thronged with strangers, seemed to take the tragic occasion as vindication, as if the city had turned out to pay tribute to his family.

One of the more improbable mourners was Alan Derecho. Katherine caught his eye just before she was escorted up the aisle to a front pew, thanks to the insistence of Emtee Dempsey. Alan's eyes met hers, and Katherine lifted her hand, pointed an index finger at him, cocked her thumb and soundlessly formed the words *Bang, bang.*

3

THREE

"THEY'RE DARLING CHILDREN," Joyce said and then, after a pause, "but how does she stand it?"

She had just emerged from the basement apartment where Lenore and her two children were ensconced, to protect them from the curious who drove past the house in Oak Park in an unending stream, to protect them from the press, who represented all the curious who couldn't take the time to go to Oak Park personally, to protect Lenore from Randy. Her brother was furious that she had not closed ranks with him and now that he could not find her, was trying unsuccessfully to convince the media that another kidnapping had taken place.

"It's part of the vendetta against the Moran family," he said darkly, looking at his interviewers with suspicious eyes.

"Have you checked out the apartment?" someone called to him.

"What apartment?"

"Where they found Marilyn Derecho and your sister."

The clip was cut off before what must have been Randy's profane reaction was broadcast.

"Such a foolish man," Emtee Dempsey commented. "For a

moment he had a modicum of moral authority, but he squandered it with all this dithering about Lenore."

The decision to invite the mother and her children to take up residence on Walton Street had been Emtee Dempsey's. Joyce had been enthusiastic about what she saw simply as more mouths to cook for. Kim kept her counsel. She alone of the three had vivid images of what the Cremona household was like and the amount of attention two small children needed. Joyce had found out about that during the past two days, not that she had altered her endorsement of the invitation. Emtee Dempsey, secure in her study, shown the children on ceremonial occasions, could quite sincerely say she enjoyed having them in the house.

"Why shouldn't she go to her brother?" Kim asked.

"I've no idea. That was her decision not ours."

True, but if Lenore's only alternative had been to stay in Oak Park, the traffic past the house would have driven her to Randy's in short order. As for Lenore herself, her manner was one of almost frightening composure.

Whenever Kim went downstairs to see if there was anything she could do to help, she found Lenore sitting on the couch reading *Little Dorrit*. The baby, asleep, lay on the couch beside her and Julia sat reading to her doll. Who would have thought that Lenore's husband was under indictment for murder and that what must have seemed her ordered and stable life was destroyed forever? Not that Lenore just lazed away the day. Joyce had brought her a ton of supplies and she had subjected the apartment to a thorough cleaning. Anyone other than Joyce might have been offended by this implied comment on the cleanliness of the household.

When Lenore put down the book to talk with Kim, her talk was only of her husband.

"He has to be very careful with his diet. Do they know that? And he is so careless about his insulin."

"He must have told them he's diabetic."

"He could just slip away, you know. In a coma. He has to be watched."

It seemed good reason to renew efforts to have Lenore permitted to see her husband. Kim felt she should admire Lenore's loyalty but found she could not, not wholeheartedly. The man whose health Lenore was concerned about had deceived her from the beginning of their marriage and announced to the world that his wife meant nothing to him.

"Is it possible she could have lived with a man, had children by him, without suspecting that he was really in love with someone else?"

Emtee Dempsey lifted her head, and the lenses of her glasses became opaque with reflected light. "I have no idea."

"It seems impossible."

It was not an opportunity the old nun was likely to pass by. She took off her glasses and rubbed her eyes.

"You must read the tales of Nathaniel Hawthorne, Sister Kimberly. The stranger with whom each of us lives is himself. That others might surprise us when the hidden depths are momentarily revealed is one thing; that we are so often startled by the self we think we know is another and far more interesting thing."

The old nun went on. They did not on that occasion return to the topic of Lenore and Joe Cremona. Donna? If anything, they all thought that the young nun, however cruelly she had exited this world, had gone to a better one, one she had been prepared to enter. Her short and truncated life had nonetheless followed a plan. No doubt, when she entered the convent she had imagined living there into extreme old age, little knowing that her life would be over in a few years. Kim almost envied her, almost, not quite.

Richard immediately guessed where Lenore was and so did Katherine Senski, but the secret was safe with them. Richard however took inordinate delight from the discovery.

"I can smell babies at a hundred paces," he claimed, nodding and smiling grimly. "Make that two hundred paces."

"Aha," said Emtee Dempsey, not caring to encourage this line.

"You should have had the house in Oak Park under surveillance," Kim said.

"It is."

"And that is how you knew of Kimberly bringing the mother and her children here."

It took some of the wind out of his sails, but in a moment he was urging them to be grateful for the unflagging attention of the police, Oak Park and Chicago, to the welfare of citizens.

"Has Joseph Cremona confessed, Richard?"

The seasoned policeman smiled at the old nun. "Murderers always plead not guilty at the trial."

"Did he kill Sister Mary Magdalene?"

"I leave that to the courts."

"No opinion?"

"It had to be him."

"He seems to be the one person involved who had no motive to harm Sister Mary Magdalene."

"What did you have against her?" Richard looked around for appreciation of his witticism. In vain.

"One can imagine her brother killing her. Or her sister."

"Don't forget her gaga mother."

"Richard!" Kim protested. She feared he would say something cruel about Emtee Dempsey next.

"Has Randy Moran denied having a key to that apartment?"

"How could he? He pays the rent."

Emtee Dempsey tucked in her chin and looked over her glasses, but Richard refused to find significance in the fact that Randy Moran as well as Joseph Cremona could have entered the apartment where Sister Mary Magdalene was held prisoner.

●

Katherine, at Emtee Dempsey's insistence, told them again of her strange experience at the Les Poupées boutique with Alan Derecho.

"You just burst in on him?" Kim asked.

"I wouldn't put it that baldly. I walked through the store, into the back, down a narrow little aisle to the door with his name on it, knocked on it and it opened."

"And you were very nearly shot. Why? Was he expecting somebody?"

"That's what I asked him."

"Surely such an establishment isn't likely to be held up, is it?"

"I doubt that."

"So what is your explanation?"

"If not money, love."

"Explain."

"Derecho has the look of a sensualist. He also has the reputation of one, as a little asking around revealed. He may have been expecting a jealous lover."

Emtee Dempsey registered this, in some sense of the term she understood it, but Kim knew that deep inside the old nun continued to marvel at the way adult human beings, creatures gifted with reason and free will, made such fools of themselves because of the flesh. As an historian, she had long known that there is a limited number of motives for the evil men do. Katherine had mentioned two, money and love. The old nun would prefer Mammon and Lust. Nor did the drama need a stage any larger than the manager's office of a boutique on the North Side.

"Can a person make a living from such a store, Katherine?"

"Apparently."

"How many employees does he have?"

"There were three salespersons in evidence the day I was there."

"Who must certainly be paid more than minimum wage."

"Sister, the price of the dresses there is enormous."

Katherine mentioned the cost of a gown, of gloves, of a scarf at the boutique, and the old nun's eyes rounded in horror.

141

"That's obscene!"

"Oh, by and large they're modest enough."

Emtee Dempsey gave Katherine a look.

Kim knew what was coming even then, although it was the following day before Emtee Dempsey proposed it.

"I've been thinking of what Katherine said."

"Oh?"

"About that boutique of Alan Derecho's."

"And you think I should drop by and see for myself."

"What a splendid idea, Sister Kimberly! You never cease to surprise me."

"It's called a preemptive strike."

"You must explain that to me sometime. And for heaven's sake be careful. Remember Katherine's experience."

Kim decided against pursuing that supposed analogy.

It was one of those occasions that would have been impossible before the order's decision to make the wearing of the habit optional. In the house on Walton Street, only Sister Mary Teresa had chosen to continue wearing the garb she had first donned as a postulant so many years ago. She had entered the Order of Martha and Mary, and the M&M's were known for their distinctive habit, particularly the massive starched headdress that made even the short and stocky Emptee Dempsey look as if she were about to engage in angelic flight. Joyce and Kim wore veils when they all went off to Mass at the cathedral each morning, but when she was on the campus at Northwestern, an A.B.D. in history, only a lapel pin would tell the knowledgeable that she was a religious. For the visit to the boutique, she slipped the lapel pin into her purse.

How dowdy she felt when she saw the dresses displayed in the window, and the feeling increased when she was inside. The salesperson, willowy, blond, wrapped in a black dress, cosmetics impasto and bright upon her face, seemed slightly taken aback by Kim, although her smile did not waver, keeping a dozen glistening perfect teeth on display. She wore a badge that bore the legend LYNN.

"May I help you?"

"I'd like to see some gloves."

Gloves seemed an inexpensive item until the blond began to lay them out on the counter and Kim managed to peek discreetly at the price. Good Lord

"These are lovely." The saleswoman was drawing on a black leather glove that reached to her elbow. She held out her arm, as if she were making shadow figures on the wall. "For afternoon as well as evening wear."

"Is Mr. Derecho in?"

She peeled the glove from her arm. If the question surprised her she gave no sign of it. If anything, she seemed less confused about Kim's presence in the store. But how was Kim to answer if she was asked what her business was. Of course this had been discussed with Emtee Dempsey.

"Give Katherine's name if they ask."

"I will not."

"Perhaps they won't ask."

"I'd rather just walk to his office and burst in as Katherine did."

"Much depends on how the question is phrased."

Kim groaned. Emtee Dempsey had an unfortunate knack of saying things just about anyone else would have considered untruths, yet she could justify such behavior in an unanswerable way. But answerable or not, Kim knew the method was wrong. Not that she was judging Sister Mary Teresa, who always admonished her to be wise as a serpent and simple as a dove.

Now, the question having been asked, Kim heard herself saying, "He will remember Katherine Senski, who called the other day."

"I remember her!" the blond cried.

"Tell him that's why I'm here."

She gave it a moment's thought. "Come," she said and led the way through the shop to the back.

The door of the manager's office was open, a man and a woman were with the man the blond identified as Derecho.

"You're busy," the blond observed.

Derecho peered at Kim, as if wondering where he had seen her before.

"Don't I know you?"

"I saw you at the funeral."

The two people with Derecho were startled by this, but he was not.

"Later," he said, addressing the blond.

She drew the door closed before taking Kim back into the store.

"Would you like some tea?"

"Is it made?"

"The water's hot. I forgot there were representatives with him. Sorry."

"Representatives?"

"Of the different lines of women's clothing."

"It was while she was dunking the tea bag in the cup of hot water Lynn had given her that Kim remembered the little man Linda had told them of.

"Did you know a representative named B. G. Briggs?"

The girl's cosmetics seemed to restrict the range of possible facial expressions, but she now wore what had to be a look of surprise. And there was an odd refocusing of her eyes.

"I'm not very good at names."

She went away then, busying herself in the shop, although everyone was being tended to. Later, when there were no customers at all, Kim was left alone with her cool tea. The man and woman representatives left, and still Kim sat on. Finally, she got up and looked around the store. Lynn was nowhere in sight. Perhaps she had gone back to see if Derecho was free now. Kim went down the narrow corridor to the back of the store. The manager's door was closed. She knocked but

144

there was no answer. She knocked several times and, mindful of Katherine's story, tried the knob. The door was locked. Kim went back to the store and asked an older clerk where Lynn was.

"Oh, she's through for the day. Could I help you?"

Kim had the sense that she could start all over again at the glove counter. She thanked the woman and left. Sitting behind the wheel of the VW she pondered her annoying experience. It seemed clear that it was her mention of B. G. Briggs that had changed the atmosphere.

FOUR

IN A PHRASE Donna had used to him, she had died to the world when she entered the convent, so maybe that was why Randy felt no additional sense of loss at her actual death. After all, he had not seen her in years. They would not let her come to the parlor grille when he visited the convent in Missouri, or she had refused to, and she had come to Chicago without letting him know. Well, she'd come and now she was dead and they were all better off because of it.

Donna herself couldn't wait to die, so that took care of her. The funeral had done much to make up for the previous attitude of the archdiocese toward the Morans. And Lenore was really better off knowing what a jerk she was married to. The only wrinkle was Lenore's refusal to come stay with him. Getting through to her proved as difficult as getting through to Donna had been. And now she had flown the coop. Where the hell could she have gone?

The taunting question tossed at him by a reporter sent Randy down to the fated apartment. It was empty, of course. He made himself a drink—a rare treat; alcohol and diabetes do not go together—and sat in the living room, tilting the blinds so that he could look south to the Sears Tower rising into a gray overcast sky. Why had he kept this apartment? A better question was why had his father kept it. Randy had checked out the rumors about Iggie and Marilyn Derecho long before they became public and had satisfied himself that they were true. He was no angel himself, but he was disgusted and shocked by his father. He could understand being attracted to Marilyn, he wouldn't have minded having a go at her himself, but for Iggie to do this was such an insult to his wife, Randy's mother, that it smacked of the unnatural. And there was the element of surprise that a man his father's age still had the itch for sex.

After Iggie died and Randy sat down with the lawyers he learned that Iggie had kept the apartment after Marilyn died. Not in his own name, of course, but his lawyers explained that his ownership was at once concealed and certain.

"He liked to go there and think," Clavell said.

Randy didn't like a goddamn lawyer knowing more about his father than he did, and he liked even less the thought of a broken-hearted Iggie Moran brooding in the apartment where his poopsie had died. He went to the apartment himself to try to figure out what the hell Iggie did there.

The closets were still full of Marilyn's clothes. It was still her place, although she was dead. Randy's worst fears were realized. His father had kept the place as a kind of shrine. Randy took particular pleasure in emptying the place of Marilyn's personal effects. He shipped it all to Alan Derecho, the son of a bitch. In the process he himself acquired the habit of hiding out at the apartment, for a few hours, for a day, rarely longer. And he had told Joe Cremona about it when his brother-in-law came to him and made the announcement that while he would be a good husband to Lenore and a good father to her children, he did not love her.

"Yeah?" Randy said. "That must be tough."

"It's my fate."

Randy had been kidding because he thought Joe must be.

What the hell was this, telling his brother-in-law a thing like that? Big deal. As for taking care of Lenore and the kids, well, he'd goddam well better. Randy would have him broken in two if he didn't. Maybe he thought Randy had gotten wind of his hanky-panky and his appearance was meant to be his defense.

"Look, Joe, I don't give a damn what you do just so it doesn't get in the papers. Know what I mean? Tell you what, I got a place you can use. If I'm there, go away, I don't want to be disturbed. Otherwise the place is yours. Just don't do anything foolish like alarm the neighbors."

Joe just stared at him while he laughed. But he was quick enough to take a key to the apartment. There was no danger of his surprising Joe there. Randy never went upstairs without checking with Horace downstairs to make sure the coast was clear. He himself had never brought a woman there. Quiet time, that's what they called it. He liked to sit there, get mildly smashed and just let whatever thought came come.

It was pretty hard now to keep thoughts of Donna from coming. How was he supposed to know that Cremona would grab Donna and lock her up? He should have known better than trust that nut with anything. Randy didn't like the thought of Cremona's trial, but it seemed a small price to pay to have everything wrapped up. He had received a call from Katherine Senski, and Moriarity too had asked if he was the only one other than Joe who had a key to the apartment. The answer was Yes, but he didn't like the implications of the question.

"Nuthin'" Horace said, when Randy asked him what he had seen during the days Donna was in the apartment. "Nuthin'. I never do."

"You never saw Cremona on the premises?"

"Never." Horace closed his eyes, rolled out his lower lip and twisted his head from side to side.

"I think you did."

"Huh?"

"Horace, I don't see how you could have missed him, know what I mean? And I think you must've been aware of all that water slopping out of that tub."

Homer followed this closely, his eyes fixed on Randy's.

"If I were you, I'd mention that, Horace. If anyone should ask."

"I already told the police I don't know nuthin'."

"I'll bet they'll ask again. Then I'd tell them."

It was the least he could do to assist the authorities in their prosecution of the man they had indicted for Donna's murder. The joke was that he had forgotten all about giving that key to Joe. There had never been any sign the guy used the apartment, but why should there be when it turned out that he had the hots for Donna and there hadn't been anything he could do about that unless she came to Chicago? That was the thought that had led him to ask Clavell to find out what he could about Wiley's motive for digging up all that old stuff on Iggie Moran. The lawyer called him that afternoon.

"We got a Trojan horse, Randy."

"How's that?"

"Your brother-in-law told Wiley Donna was a witness to Marilyn Derecho's death, that she knew her father had done it. Get her to Chicago and he could make the charge stick."

"He believed that?"

The prosecutor's ultimate goal was to get the Moran wealth declared ill-gotten gains, and the only one that would really hurt was Randy. Geez. And so he had another little talk with Horace about what the condominium manager had seen at the apartment.

5

BENJAMIN RUSH DID not like the law used in a tactical way, suits threatened without a firm intention to pursue them if the opposite party did not crumble. One should only go to law with serious intent. Of late, he had the impression that too many of his fellow lawyers were engaging in a species of blackmail, and he had never had this sense more strongly than in the case of Moran against the Archdiocese of Chicago. It could be said that the archdiocese had invited the assault of young Randolph Moran by impugning the reputation of his late father, and that his lawyers were well advised to move to preserve the good name of Ignatius Moran. It could be said and it could be believed were it not for the fact that the Moran lawyers, Clavell, Catesby and Tribe, were notorious as representatives of clients on the shady side of the law. And the late Ignatius Moran had been their most notable client.

Rush had never had the dubious pleasure of meeting Iggie Moran. Most of the man's interests had been in professional sports, lake shipping, contracting and outdoor advertising, all perfectly legitimate enterprises from which, by all reports, Moran realized an enormous personal income. On the face of it, it seemed improbable that a successful businessman would become associated, rightly or wrongly, with questionable dealings. Perhaps if he had not won so many contracts with the city of Chicago he would have been spared the kind of scrutiny that gained him the reputation of one skirting the edge of legality, perhaps veering across the line into outright criminality. But none of the charges of bribing and kickbacks had ever stuck, and Benjamin Rush was as opposed to flimsy indictments by the grand jury as he was of harassment by civil suit. But, in the old adage, enough mud had been thrown for some of it to stick, and Iggie Moran had acquired an unsavory reputation. Moreover, the man seemed almost to glory in it. Rush had memorable images of Iggie triumphantly meeting the press after yet another effort to prove him guilty of something had failed. He never seemed more guilty than when his innocence had been established.

"Then you think he was a criminal?" Emtee Dempsey asked in her unfortunately abrupt manner.

"What I think is of little consequence. Being a criminal is not a status conferred on a person by private opinion. It must be established by a court of law . . ."

But the great headdress was swaying and her finger was waggling. "No lecture, Benjamin, please. I think I have a rough understanding of the Constitution."

"There were many efforts during his lifetime to convict him of criminal activities. None of them was successful. The posthumous effort seems to have dissolved with the death of Donna Moran."

Harrington, retired prosecutor and fellow member at Cliff Dwellers, seated next to Rush in the library of the club, had shaken his head in disapproval when the matter of Wiley's attempt to in effect bring Iggie to trial some years after his death was raised.

"Strictly *entre nous*," Harrington whispered, and others in the library stirred, "the whole thing was largely based on the assurance that the Moran daughter would implicate her father in the death of Marilyn Derecho as well as in the drug traffic."

"Who could have given such an assurance?"

" 'Another member of the family.' We now know who that was."

"Joe Cremona."

"Exactly. The romantic brother-in-law."

"And murderer?"

" 'Each man kills the thing he loves,' " Harrington intoned, throwing back his head and discontinuing the failed effort to whisper. Benjamin Rush realized that his friend was about to draw on his enormous reservoir of memorized verse. " 'The coward does it with a kiss, the brave man with a sword.' "

"How do you characterize one who does it by drowning?"

"Not as a Baptist," Harrington said, with a twinkle in his eye. "In any case, it seems clear that Cremona used the prosecutor to get his beloved back to Chicago."

That a man should retain a passion for a woman after she has entered the convent and given herself to God was incomprehensible to Bejamin Rush. Harrington, perhaps predictably, was of another mind.

"I stand in awe of such single-minded devotion. I ask myself if there is anything I care enough about to kill for."

"Killing the one you supposedly care about seems self-contradictory."

"You must have learned by now how little life has to do with logic."

"You said the case largely depended on the hope Donna Moran would give evidence against her family. What else was there?"

Harrington's eyes lifted theatrically and went out of sight behind his lids. "Ah, Benjamin, there are rumors and rumors about rumors. Nothing you or I would consider a basis for prosecution."

Harrington touched his lips with a long index finger and permitted his eyes to dart back and forth.

Emtee Dempsey, to whom he conveyed the gist of this Delphic conversation, began to tell him a story of a pope who had dug up his predecessor and put him on trial, something Benjamin Rush permitted himself to disbelieve. It did seem a ghoulish enough parallel, however, which he supposed was his old friend's reason for telling it. Now Wiley had Cremona himself to prosecute and what had begun as a vendetta against the Moran family had turned them into objects of sympathy. The cardinal, conveniently out of town when Donna was buried, finding that the public mood had changed, was photographed thanking Randy Moran for his family's generous support of the Church over so many years. He extended his personal condolences to the Morans over the tragic loss of Sister Mary Magdalene Moran.

"Does this mean the archdiocese will receive the million Ignatius Moran left?" Sister Mary Teresa asked.

"That's unclear. Randy withdrew the offer in a huff and there is no mention that he offered it anew."

six

LINDA LAY AWAKE thinking of B. G. Briggs. The drowned nun had been given a real send-off but poor little Briggs was shipped back to St. Louis like any other cargo and had probably been consigned to the earth or the crematory oven without ceremony. Well, that was far more typical than a jammed cathedral, all the media in attendance, a police escort to the cemetery.

Georgie had balked about going to the cemetery.

"What the hell for?"

"To satisfy our morbid public."

Linda shared his reluctance. To that point, you had to take it on trust that the body of the young nun was at the center of all the folderol. The coffin had been closed at the funeral home, it was covered with a large white cloth and wheeled up the aisle of the cathedral; it was wheeled out again and slid into a hearse. It all had to do with death, but abstractly. At the cemetery there was a hole in the ground into which they would put the box containing the dead body of Donna Moran.

It made you think. Of what? Of Briggs, apparently. Thank God, things had not gone any farther with him than they had.

She had been willing, she could admit that to herself. She had actually been looking forward to getting a room at the Palmer House and enjoying a little hanky-panky with the clothing salesman. Kid stuff. But what if they had and now he was dead. It would be as if part of her were gone, dead, buried. Or, worse, reduced to ash.

Would she feel that way when her ex-husbands died? Somehow it wasn't the same thing. It had been a while since either of them anyway, and too many negative memories canceled out tenderness. Now there was a grim thought, that you could like people only to the degree that you don't know them well.

She and Georgie had gone on to the cemetery, the hole in the ground was prettied up, the mounds of earth covered with blankets of artificial grass, the abundance of flowers out of season denying the presence of death.

"Know who that is?" Katherine Senski asked her when they were walking back to their parked cars.

Katherine hunched a shoulder at a man whose hands were plunged into the pockets of a top coat whose collar was pulled up and who was tiptoeing toward the road, small steps, then a long one, avoiding the mud and puddles of standing water.

"No."

"Marilyn Derecho's brother."

Only later did the oddity of his being there strike her, and she wished she had quizzed Katherine about it. The fact that the veteran reporter had drawn attention to Alan Derecho suggested that she too found it significant. Otherwise, it was possible to think that he had known his sister's friend before she entered the convent and his presence was a tribute to that. Or so she might have left it if she hadn't got half soused talking about Briggs with Georgie.

"Look at it this way, sweetie. Just the fact that you accepted the date meant a lot to him. I could tell."

Georgie was a darling. Linda knew he was probably lying about Briggs's reaction, but it was a nice thought that this lonely traveling man had gone to his death knowing that . . . Knowing what? That some femme fatale was waiting for him? Linda had shed all delusions about herself, or so she thought. The wild hopes that she had taken into two marriages had been so definitively dashed that she had to fight cynicism night and day. What had she thought of Briggs alive?

At O'Hare he had been at first a pest and then a chance to redeem the situation at least in part. His huffing and puffing once he realized he was being interviewed had struck her as comic, and when he came to Walton Street the next day still clutching his shoulder bag, as if he'd slept with it, and complained that she had put him in danger of his life, she had thought him absurd. But cute too and she had agreed to meet him at the Palmer House.

"He was right, Georgie. He was in danger."

"Yeah."

"Georgie, who shot him?"

Georgie was about as interested in that question as the police were. Richard Moriarity was being visibly patient when she got in to see him, her motives there a little mixed as she would not have told even Georgie.

"You gotta know how many murders a day we have in this city."

"But he wasn't mugged, was he?"

He sighed and called for the report, then flipped through it, as if it were a magazine he did not want to read. Briggs's wallet, credit cards, cash, had been found on the body. That is why they had identified him so easily.

"Where exactly was the body found?"

He read off the address in a bored voice. Linda would not have thought she was attracted to redheads, but this guy didn't have the pale freckled skin that often goes with red hair, and he seemed bigger than he was, filling his office, the man in charge.

"He told me he had an appointment at ten o'clock."

"He was shot about eleven."

"So he must have kept his appointment. Didn't he have an appointment book."

Richard Moriarity shook his head.

"Was his shoulder bag found?"

"He lose one?"

"That's my question."

In her memories of him, Briggs was always gripping the strap of that bag and pressing it against his side with his arm.

"It wasn't with the luggage he left at the Stevenson."

"He carried it around with him. It had his initials on it."

There was no record of the shoulder bag in the papers Moriarity ruffled through. But if Briggs had been robbed, why was he shot? And not just shot but riddled with bullets?

Lieutenant Moriarity again flipped through the printout. "He was clean as a whistle here and in St. Louis. What's your interest?"

She might have told him she was cooling her heels in the Palmer House for several hours while Briggs lay dead of gunshot wounds, but she didn't.

"Just doing my job. I should think you would appreciate that."

"Hey, I'm not criticizing. Good for you." He leaned toward her. God, what shoulders. "Linda, it's a damned shame but it's true. Few murders are solved. You know the phrase, getting away with murder. It ought to be retired. People are getting away with murder every day."

"Not me."

He grinned. Behind him on a table was a picture of a woman and three redheaded kids. Linda felt watched. She got up.

"Thanks. Lieutenant Moriarity."

"You're welcome, Ms. Pastorini. You any relation to the football player?"

"No, the wrestler."

It was there between them as they stood grinning at each other, but she turned and left and that was that. She was not going to get interested in a married man.

But B. G. Briggs had been married. She couldn't get the way he hung on to his shoulder bag out of her mind. Muggers would have noticed that. But why kill him? Why shoot him as often as they had? A twisted kind of mercy? She shuddered at the image of Briggs lurching about as all those bullets tore into his body.

He had been employed by F. X. Nicolo Creations, and Linda called the Chicago office three times before she got something other than an answering device. "Yeah?" a voice said.

"F. X. Nicolo Creations?"

"Who's this?"

"Linda Pastorini with Cable News—"

The phone went dead. What the hell. Linda dialed again, but after several rings a recording asked her to leave a message after the buzzer sounded. After the buzzer sounded she made a vulgar noise and hung up the phone. She flipped open the directory again and scribbled the address of F. X. Nicolo Creations and, since Georgie wasn't around, drove her own car to the near North Side address.

7

SEVEN

JOYCE AND KIM took Julia and the baby to the zoo while Lenore tried unsuccessfully to get in to visit her husband. Cremona refused to see her. The first time she was rebuffed she came back to Walton Street weeping hysterically, but she just kept stoically at it and they watched the kids while she tried, but her husband would not see her.

"Why does she want to see the creep?" Joyce asked.

"He's her husband."

"So? Donna was her sister. And he publicly announced that he didn't love his wife, he loved her sister."

The trouble with Joyce's reaction was that Kim could all too easily imagine Joyce acting exactly as Lenore was if she were in the same fix. The desire to forgive is so powerful it almost seems a temptation, as if the motive for it were suspect, but surely it is admirable in a wife to stick with her husband even when he has been untrue to her. Spouses must reconcile with their adulterous mates all the time, although admittedly outright adultery seemed a lesser infidelity than Joe Cremona's toward Lenore.

"Maybe she just wants to get away from the kids, Joyce."

"Yeah."

The theory was that they loved having Lenore and her children living in the basement apartment of the house on Walton Street. Lenore seemed to like the basement apartment well enough, although she kept cleaning it from top to bottom, concerned lest her children come into contact with strange germs. Joyce happily supplied cleaning materials and would have been happy to pitch in, little as she thought the apartment needed such spring cleaning treatment, but Lenore said she would do it herself.

"Therapy?" Kim asked.

"Spoken like a woman who seldom cleans house."

"Why then?"

"Therapy. I have the right to say it."

The nuns might have been tempted to discourage Lenore's efforts to see Joe, but that would have been salt in the wound, given the likelihood that he would refuse to see her anyway. Besides, it was good to see Lenore behind the wheel of her car, in charge, driving away as if she had important errands to run.

"How would she feel about him if he treated her nicely?" Joyce asked.

"We'll never know."

That Joe Cremona was awaiting trial and thus might be presumed innocent still was lost on the newspapers as much as on anyone else, and the imprisoned man's refusal to own up to his guilt was taken to be a predictable ploy dictated by his lawyers. Psychologists from several local universities concurred that Cremona's leading of the police and media to the scene of the crime was a common phenomenon, a suppressed desire to be caught and punished, no matter his continued insistence that he had nothing to do with Donna Moran's death. A little bow of a smile on one professor's mouth suggested that few things men do had the capacity to surprise her.

"Yes," she said, when reminded of Cremona's near nervous breakdown when the body was found.

"Doesn't that suggest he was surprised?"

"On the conscious level, perhaps. He may have driven so far underground the deed he'd done that he was genuinely surprised. On the conscious level."

"You're sure he's guilty?"

"Guilty?" The corners of her mouth wavered, then resumed their upward tilt. "That is out of my field."

"I thought guilt was a psychological phenomenon."

"In that sense of the term, we're all guilty."

Emtee Dempsey groaned as she zapped the interview with the remote control. "If that woman were speaking of Original Sin, she might make some sense."

Did that mean Emtee Dempsey considered Joe Cremona guilty?

"Of Original Sin? Of course."

"Lenore says Joe didn't do it," Joyce said.

"Did you ask her?"

"I was downstairs when the radio was on and someone referred to 'Joe Cremona, the murderer of the Carmelite nun' and then right away said, 'Alleged murderer.' And Lenore said, 'That's right. Alleged.' So I asked her if she thought he was innocent and she said she knew he was."

Kim wondered if Lenore really believed that. Of course, she would want to believe it, just as she would want to believe that Joe never said those things about not loving her and always loving her sister, Donna. Imagine what lay before the poor woman. A prolonged sensational trial, her husband sent away to prison, and she left alone with two children to raise. Eventually, she would have to accept Randy's help. Not that she would ever be wanting for things material, given her share of the Moran wealth. But that would be small consolation as she faced a lonely future.

The aged Mrs. Moran lived in a plush nursing home, receiving the best care money could buy, but that would not give her back her mental capacities. Kim had taken Lenore to see her mother one day and had left them alone minutes after they went to the old woman's room, not to grant them privacy but to spare herself the pain of a mother seeing her daughter as a stranger and a daughter unable to pour out her sorrows to her mother. Told of the episode, Emtee Dempsey gave Lenore a rosary and advised her to invoke the aid of her Heavenly Mother, but there was no sign Lenore had ever said her beads. The rosary lay on a table in the downstairs apartment precisely where Lenore had put it when it was first given her.

Lenore couldn't see her husband, but finally she and her brother Randy got together. He agreed to talk to Joe for her and Randy got in to see his brother-in-law.

"Did he ask about the kids?"

"He's not himself."

"Did you give him the cookies?"

What a fuss Lenore had made, baking for Joe, and she was delighted to hear Randy describe his reception of them. It turned out Randy was lying. Joe wanted no connection at all with his wife.

"What about his insulin?"

"I gave it to him."

Lenore and her children had been with them two weeks when Richard showed up on their doorstep.

"She in?" he asked, when Kim answered the door.

He meant Emtee Dempsey. "Yes."

"She heard?"

"Heard what?"

"I only want to say it once."

Kim hurried after him as he strode down the hall to the study, his gait that of a man going to his doom. He took two steps into the study and stopped.

"He's dead."

It was what in theatrical talk is called a slow take. Emtee Dempsey's pen stopped moving across the page, her head raised and her eyes gradually focused on Richard and Kim standing just behind him.

"I beg your pardon."

"He's dead. Cremona. I thought I'd bring the news myself."

He walked over to a chair and slumped into it. "What a helluva thing. The media will have the time of their lives."

"Dead of what cause, Richard?"

"Dead because he shot enough poison into himself to kill half the cell block." He made a face. "And don't ask me how he got it. They can handle questions like that at the lockup."

"What kind of poison."

"The guess is hydrochloric acid."

Emtee Dempsey rose slowly but it was to Kim she spoke. "Sister, go to Lenore."

FIVE

KATHERINE SENSKI HAD reached an age when the follies of men had lost their capacity to surprise her. Certainly in retrospect it seemed all but inevitable that a man like Joe Cremona, who had manipulated an otherwise sensible prosecutor into luring Donna Moran to Chicago, was single-minded enough both to kill her when she failed to cooperate with his fantasies and then kill himself when his world collapsed around him.

"It is quite certain that he killed himself?" Emtee Dempsey spoke with impatience.

"The hydrochloric acid was in a toilet cleaner. There was none in his cell, only in the common rest room, and he wasn't allowed to use that."

"Never?"

"The shower, but not the rest room. He had a toilet in his cell."

"Then how could he have gotten hold of the cleaner?"

"No other prisoner is likely to tell. One of the trustees might have brought it to him."

"And then taken it away?"

Katherine shrugged. Cremona had injected it into himself, reusing the syringe he was permitted as a diabetic.

"God rest his soul."

"Amen," responded Katherine Senski.

Katherine bowed her head and tried not to have images of purgatory that were too vivid or, worse, the other place. There were those who refused to accept the morality of penning up, even temporarily, undoubted criminals; such a mind-set could scarcely comprehend the notion of eternal punishment. Katherine Senski believed in hell, both as a matter of faith and reason, but it was a part of her religion not to imagine any particular person there, not Stalin, not Caligula, not the many mass butchers of the twentieth century. There was always the chance of last moment repentance, as Dante stressed. It was one thing to think of Joe Cremona as guilty of the murder of Sister Mary Magdalene, née Donna Moran. It was quite another to think of him as damned.

A great hullabaloo would go up on the part of those who thought it beyond belief that such a thing could happen in a well-run jail. Katherine did not agree. A murder can be committed in church, to say nothing of a jail, and it is impossible to have sufficient safeguards against the occurrence. But the prevention of suicide was yet more impossible. Someone determined to make an exit from this world is very hard to detain.

"Perhaps he belonged to the Hemlock Society," Emtee Dempsey said.

"And what is that?"

"A group formed to agitate for the human right to kill oneself. A right that must be implemented by the doctor if the person himself is incapable of it, perhaps comatose. The doctor is obliged, according to the theory, to administer a lethal dose of morphine, the right is exercised, and the person shuffles off this mortal coil."

"How dreadful."

"You had better say, how pagan. No, in antiquity it was not

168

rare to find even wise men—Seneca—who professed to find something noble in a well-executed suicide. When pain or debility or ennui overwhelmed, one let the blood out of his veins and that was that. There were, however, dissenting pagan voices, notably Socrates. He was urged to cheat the executioner and take his own life, but he was repelled by the suggestion, stating that he belonged to God, not to himself, and thus could not so dispose of another's property. It is the socratic view that is reinforced by Christianity. In this post-Christian age, the resurgence of pagan attitudes toward life and death is just what we should expect. But I don't suppose Joe Cremona was a professing pagan."

"He was a star-crossed lover, at least in his own eyes."

All this was pretty abstract talk to be going on in the same house in which the new widow was being consoled by Joyce and Kim.

When Kim had gone down to the basement apartment, Lenore might have thought she was about to get relief from her children. Instead, she was given the news about her husband. Her shriek brought Emtee Dempsey to her feet, and she lay her hand on the pages containing her account of Bernard of Clairvaux's preaching of a crusade, as if they were in danger. Her brows rose above her round metal framed glasses as she exchanged a look with Richard. The old nun was a pillar of strength, calm in nearly every storm, but she had her limitations. She could not abide the sight or sound of an hysterical woman. That is why the younger nuns consoled Lenore in the basement apartment, where they alternated between calming the mother and soothing her children. Richard left and Emtee Dempsey was happy to receive Katherine's visit.

"I look forward to your story on his final days, Katherine. You have the great gift of putting matters before the eyes of your reader."

"It is my profession."

"I understand that. But I never have the same sense of being there when I read other journalists. Composition of place, Saint Ignatius called it."

Katherine decided against pursuing that allusion. And she was grateful for the old nun's praise. If she still wrote such stories—she could have confined herself to her thrice weekly column, ruminating about what she would—it was to provide a model for younger reporters. And some not so young. There was a bad tendency nowadays for the reporter to report on himself, making the news an aspect of autobiography. Katherine had been raised in the school that saw the reporter as the Recording Angel, interested only in what had happened, to whom, where and why. The writer came into it not at all.

The block in which Joe Cremona's cell was found led off from a central area where an officer sat before the bank of monitors that gave him a view of the various divisions of his responsibility. By and large, the screens showed the featureless expanse of a corridor lined with cells. There was a table in the area across which visitors could speak to a prisoner, but this was not a privilege accorded to Joe Cremona. If this had been intended as further punishment, it was pointless. He had expressed his wish to see no one. An officer named Paul Dudley had kept after him, but Cremona refused to speak to Lenore even through the bars. He had relented in the case of Randy Moran, however, and received several visits from his brother-in-law.

"Maybe because Moran always brought him a Coke," Dudley told Katherine.

"How do you mean?"

"He was a Cokeaholic. God knows how many he drank a day."

"So Randy Moran took him a can of Coke."

"We all did. Me, other officers, his lawyer. The Coke alone should've killed him."

Dudley was anything but apologetic about the toilet cleaner. "Look, no matter what we do, there's complaints. We do nothing about the jakes, we got do-gooders describing the place as if it were Devil's Island. We make 'em clean their toilets, there's those who say we should be paying them for it. We want monitors in the cells, the ACLU goes crazy, insisting on the right to privacy of these guys. Now you will probably write that we are delinquent and should have seen what Cremona was up to."

Dudley sat at his desk in the high bright room with his bank of monitors, on the wall a large legible clock whose minute hand lurched from position to position, a Coke machine near the door. He might have been a character in an existentialist play.

Katherine asked those in the cells around Cremona's if they knew anything. Looking into those unblinking stares convinced her there was little point in asking if they lamented the death of a man accused of murdering a Carmelite nun.

"What happens to Lenore and her children now?"

Emtee Dempsey looked at her. "In a sense, nothing has changed. Her husband was never coming back to her anyway. Now at least she is spared his going through a trial."

"That seems a small blessing."

"You're absolutely certain that it was suicide, Katherine?"

"Absolutely certain? How could I be?"

"Does your story contain a complete list of his visitors?"

Katherine had written that the lawyer assigned to Cremona, Lance Wiggins, had been to see him several times, raising hell about the need to consult his client through the bars of his cell. The complaint was for the record, according to Dudley. Wiggins would give his client his best shot, but he was not wild about gaining publicity as the counsel of the man who killed the Carmelite nun. Wiley, the prosecutor, had been to see Cremona. And his brother-in-law.

"Randy Moran visited Joe Cremona."

"Twice."

"Why didn't you mention that in your story?"

"That is not, God willing, the last story I shall write, Sister Mary Teresa."

2

THE BUILDING HAD been a warehouse that an enterprising developer restored, using little more than the shell and the steel understructure to create an attractive multipurpose building. F. X. Nicolo Creations was located in a boutique situated off what had once been a loading ramp. Linda came along the ramp, liking the echoing sound her boots made on the timbered surface that might have been artificially distressed to create an impression of age. But the age was real and the scars and gouges in the ramp had been made by honest-to-God loading and unloading.

One of the large doors was now all glass with a revolving door set in it, and Linda came into a high-ceilinged hall on the right side of which in plastic letters lifting off the wall was the indication that she had come to the right place. F. X. NICOLO in blood red letters raised off a chalk white wall to the left of glass doors. By contrast, the name of the boutique was modestly spelled in small charcoal letters. LES POUPEES. It didn't seem the sort of place that would use an answering machine.

The door did not give when she pushed. Locked? It was

two-thirty in the afternoon, surely part of the business day in the dress industry. Linda cupped her hands and peered through the glass at the white carpet, at counters featuring gloves and scarves and stockings. Through an open door at the back she saw white office furniture, metal framed pictures of anorexic models displaying the latest fashions. On the desk was the answering machine, its lights all aglow. Where the hell was the man who had answered?

She stepped back from the door and looked around, a half smile on her face, ready to share with any witness her amusement at finding herself confronting a locked door. But she was alone. Across the wide airy area were two doors separated by an interval, PDQ Direct Mail and Studio Audrey.

In the first of these, Linda found half a dozen women seated at large tables, stuffing envelopes with mechanical boredom. All eyes were on her, but they went on filling the envelopes.

"Help you?"

Frizzy hair at the sides of his head, an enormous belly straining against the buttons of his shirt, the engaging smile of a loser.

"What do you know of F. X. Nicolo Creations?"

"Across the way?" His smile had gone from hopeful to disappointed.

"Yes."

"Nothing."

"How many people work there?"

"Look, I said nothing. I meant it. I've got enough to keep me busy here." He glanced over his shoulder and the pace of envelope stuffing increased slightly.

"They don't answer their phone."

"Check with the phone company."

Linda tried Studio Audrey, a pleasant place filled with odd but pleasant smells, a one-woman commercial art enterprise, Audrey being the one woman. She spun away from her drawing board to face Linda and immediately one eye narrowed and her head tipped.

"I know you."

"You're Audrey?"

"Linda Pastorini! Right? Channel whatever?"

"I hope you can help me out, Audrey."

She wore a blue smock, and when she stood she was nearly six feet tall. She was delighted to have what she considered a celebrity right there in her studio.

"I watch you all the time."

"Did you happen to see an interview I did with a man named Briggs?"

Something happened to her face and her eyes avoided Linda's "Briggs."

"He represented the company across the way. The dress manufacturer."

"Oh, they don't manufacture anything. They represent a number of lesser Italian lines. They're just middlemen."

"They?"

"Him. He owns the boutique too. The Poops."

"Briggs sold for him."

She sat down again and moved back and forth in a thirty-degree arc in her swivel chair.

"Briggs was killed," she said.

"Yes."

She lifted her chin and looked Linda in the eye. "I knew Briggs." A moment of silence. "I didn't know he was married."

"Neither did I," Linda said softly.

That was the Open Sesame, they were two women half ashamed to have succumbed to the minor key of B. G. Briggs's charm.

"Would you like some coffee?"

She made a fresh pot, and within five minutes they might have been old friends. Audrey agreed that it wasn't fair that the death of Briggs should have been banished to oblivion while the admittedly sad death of Donna Moran dominated local news coverage.

174

"I mean they were both murdered. Her we know why, but Briggs? What did he ever do to anyone? He was really upset when my interview with him appeared. And appeared and appeared. He looked me up to say I'd endangered him and I thought he was being overly dramatic."

"What was he afraid of?"

"He said Iggie Moran."

"Don't you believe him?"

"Iggie Moran is dead."

"So the Moran family, then."

"Earlier when I called F. X. Nicolo Creations someone answered. A man. Would that have been F. X.?"

Audrey shrugged. "I suppose. I never see but one man over there regularly. He was there when I moved in, but we're not really all that chummy, the three of us in this part of the building. And I'm not likely to shop in The Poops. Anyway I'm in and out a lot myself."

Audrey solicited business, did the art work and delivered it when it was done, which would indeed keep her on the run. She showed Linda some of her work, technical things, involving airbrushes, very impressive.

"How did you meet Briggs?"

"He saw me working here and looked in." A little smile formed on her lips as she remembered.

"Do other representatives come here?"

She thought about it. "Briggs came to Chicago maybe twice a month that I knew of and sometimes we went out. You know how short he was, it never seemed really serious, but he was a lot of fun."

Linda did not pry. What did it matter anyway if Audrey had done what she herself had been ready to do?

"That often? Once a month?"

"Once we went out with Briggs's boss."

"F. X. Nicolo? What was he like?"

All Audrey knew was that they had fun.

"Just the three of you?"

Audrey fell silent.

"Who do you think killed Briggs, Audrey?"

The question surprised her. "How would I know?"

"You must have gotten to know him pretty well."

"Well, he sure wasn't worried about anyone killing him, I know that much. It must have been what he said, the Morans."

After she left Audrey, Linda sat in her car looking at the remodeled warehouse. Maybe talking to F. X. Nicolo would be no more productive than talking to Audrey, but she'd like to ask him about the time he and Briggs had gone out on the town with Audrey.

3

THREE

"I TELL MYSELF I'll never see him again," Lenore said, holding her baby tightly against her. "But I can't believe it." Julia looked up at her mother wide-eyed, finally affected by the disruption in the even tenor of their days—a move to this basement apartment on Walton Street, now her mother strangely stoic at the loss of her husband.

Walton Street was meant to be a sanctuary, a privileged place. But Lenore would know her sister had come here with the same expectation and now Donna was dead. Donna was dead and Joe as well, the deaths connected in a bizarre way.

"Our seventh anniversary is next month."

Kim put Julia on her own knee. Lenore had a way of saying things to which there was no reply.

"Till death do us part," Lenore murmured and a dry sob shook her.

"Do you know Alan Derecho?" Kim surprised herself. Like Lenore, she was just saying things.

"Why?"

"He came to Sister Mary Magdalene's funeral."

Lenore sat forward, clutching her baby more firmly, and it began to cry.

"Donna would never go out with him!"

"Yeah. I saw him there," Richard said when Kim put it to him in Emtee Dempsey's office.

"Did they know each other?"

Richard smiled at Emtee Dempsey, a not-quite-condescending smile. "What made you interested in Derecho?"

"I got an odd reception when I dropped into his boutique," Katherine said.

"How so?"

"He aimed a gun at me."

"C'mon."

"I am perfectly serious. He was more frightened than I was, but that didn't make it any more pleasant."

Kim saw no reason to tell Richard of her own visit to the boutique. Any initial skepticism he had shown at Katherine's account suddenly vanished. He looked over both shoulders with exaggerated drama. "I know nothing I say here will get beyond these walls. Let me tell you about Alan Derecho."

Before she let him begin, Emtee Dempsey wanted tea brought in.

"Perhaps Richard would like something more bracing," Katherine said.

Meaning she wanted a glass of sherry, but Kim wished Katherine had accepted tea. Richard's drinking always made her nervous because of the Moriarity track record in matters of alcohol, even though Richard himself seemed to have no special problem. On the other hand, he had never in her experience refused a drink, nor did he refuse now. When he settled back to tell them about Alan Derecho he was accordingly in an expansive mood, bringing the wider world to these secluded ladies, an attitude Katherine might have resented if she weren't enjoying her sherry as much as Richard enjoyed his beer.

The Derechos were a second-generation Chilean-American

family, their immigration stemming from Marilyn and Alan's grandfather's appointment as Chilean consul to Chicago. Before his second term was over, he resigned, applied for citizenship and settled in Chicago in the import-export business, providing a commercial bridge between his old country and his new, to everyone's satisfaction and to his own enrichment. His son Enrique took over the business at a time when political affairs in Chile were turbulent and his father's contacts were either being shot out of or aging out of active life. He expanded the business to a general Latin American one but never recovered the level his father had achieved in the first days of the enterprise. Marilyn and Alan had been born into the lap of relative luxury, their Latin origin an intriguing difference rather than an ethnic minus, but as they grew and the family slowly descended the economic scale, they found themselves confused with the Chicano subpopulation of migrant workers. There had been money enough to send Marilyn to the M&M college, but just barely, and when she entered Northwestern Law School it was as part of a minority quota. And, allegedly, thanks to a subsidy from Iggie Moran. Alan took over the business, and in his hands it again prospered though doubts had been raised as to whether women's fashions could account for his apparent income.

"What do you mean?" Emtee Dempsey asked.

"Let me put it this way. One of the things the prosecutor tried to pin on Iggie Moran was involvement with drugs. A good part of the case would have relied on a mysterious informer."

"Derecho."

"In part. The father, not the son."

Alan's father had presided over the decline of the business and had marveled at his son's prosperity. Wonder gave way to suspicion. The conclusion seemed inescapable that Alan had taken the family business across the line into the illegal and the criminal.

"He said this?"

Richard frowned, began to say something, paused. Finally, "He is said to have said it. He wouldn't write it down in advance of the trial, he wouldn't record it. In the end it didn't matter."

Derecho's daughter, Marilyn, died of a drug overdose in what was described as a love nest, Iggie Moran publicly reformed, and the elder Derecho took up residence in a monastery in Elmira, New York, wanting to live his last years in a religious atmosphere that would ease his memories.

Richard was not unaware of the effect of his account, and his voice grew measured as he brought it to an end. There was silence in the study.

"And has Alan too reformed?" Emtee Dempsey asked.

"His only crime was missing Iggie Moran when he tried to run him down."

"But he is prosperous?"

"Lots of merchants are prosperous."

Richard had said all he intended to say, much to the old nun's annoyance. Emtee Dempsey had appreciated his sketch of the fall of the houses of Derecho and Moran, but Kim knew that at the forefront of the old nun's mind was the fact that a guest of hers had been abducted and killed and now the presumed killer was himself dead. Others might find in this a closing of the circle, but Emtee Dempsey seemed to share Lenore's wonder. Who would be next?

After Richard had gone and Katherine and Kim and Emtee Dempsey were alone in the study—Joyce was in the basement apartment helping Lenore with her children, trying to distract her with the boxing matches on ESPN—Kim mentioned what Lenore had said and, sure enough, the old nun nodded. She nodded for some time, but she said nothing. Katherine adopted a patient expression.

"The man who kidnapped and killed Sister Mary Magdalene has committed suicide," she said. "He is not likely to harm anyone else."

It was infuriating, for Kim if not for Katherine, that Emtee

Dempsey did not contest this in words, but her whole manner suggested that she had deep doubts about so neat an account. If only she would say something, Kim could ask her if she imagined that one of Joe Cremona's visitors had filled him full of poison. Katherine, thank God, put the question.

"Surely you don't think Joe Cremona died by any other hand than his own, Sister Mary Teresa?"

"Given his romantic motivation, I cannot imagine him doing such a thing without leaving a lengthy explanation behind. Or was there a note?"

"Think of what the man had on his conscience, Sister."

"Had he seen the chaplain?"

Here was a question Kim could answer. Dudley had been emphatic. Joe Cremona had specified that he wanted to see no priest, minister, rabbi, guru or psychologist. God had taken Donna from him twice, and he had no desire for any further relations with the deity.

"But he did have visits from Randy Moran."

"Sister," Katherine said, "no one else poisoned him. Cremona injected the poison himself."

Sister Mary Teresa let the topic go, and they chatted of other things until it was time for Katherine to go. Kim locked the front door after letting Katherine out, stopped in the kitchen and listened to the sounds of television in the apartment below. The fights were still on, apparently. She had work to do in her room but before going upstairs went back to the study to see if Sister Mary Teresa wanted anything.

"I should talk with Randy Moran, I suppose," the old nun said in tones of resignation.

"What for?"

"Sister, pleasant as it is for us, we cannot keep Lenore and her children here indefinitely. She and her brother are going to have to work something out, and it will be better if I am on friendly terms with him."

It seemed best to let it go at that.

F O U R

"I WANT TO talk to you about the death of Joe Cremona," Moriarity had said on the phone, and Randy Moran appreciated the directness. For one thing, it gave him a chance to get his ducks in a row before the detective lieutenant arrived. Randy instructed the receptionist to send him right in, no delays. He didn't intend to play games, although God knows he had a busy enough day.

Cremona's death was one kind of business for the police and quite another for Randy. In his last days, Iggie had tried to imagine and cover every future contingency his family might face, and sure enough there was a provision covering the loss of a spouse by any of them. That money, added to the amount that had been set aside in an escrow account for Donna, in case she ever left the convent, made for some very complicated but very interesting legal and financial problems. He and Lenore were suddenly a lot richer than they had been.

Lenore had always been the oddball of the family. The middle child, she was somehow convinced she wasn't loved as much as Randy and Donna. She was right, and the way she acted thinking so, made it worse. Iggie had preferred to get

182

news of how things were going with Lenore indirectly, from Randy or Donna. He had doted on Donna, and she had let him down by becoming a nun. He had gone to bat for Randy, taking the blame when his drunken son drove his car through a storefront. Randy always thought Lenore should have been Iggie's favorite: in some strange way she was more like him than Donna or himself. Donna had been shocked to learn how her father became wealthy; Randy had decided to enjoy the spoils, whatever their origin. But Lenore, he could imagine her doing whatever Iggie had done and not batting an eye.

"I hate a whiner," he said to Randy.

Randy had never thought of Lenore as a whiner. More like the ghost at the banquet. She liked to stay in the background wearing a sad accusing expression. Have fun. Don't mind me. Randy had been relieved when Cremona switched to Lenore after Donna entered the convent. Why? Lenore was as attractive as Donna and Cremona was no prize. But Lenore had cast herself in the role of the ugly sister, Cinderella. She refused to go to college, although Iggie would have sent her anywhere she wanted to go. Donna had been dreaming of the M&M since grade school, the family made a fuss of her ambition, and Lenore acted as if her young sister had pre-empted that route. The crazy ideas Lenore had!

She actually took the examination to be admitted to the police force and would have been a shoo-in, what with affirmative action, women's rights, not to mention Iggie's pull, and she scored high, but after basic training she lost interest in the idea, maybe because Iggie had backed her against her mother. Florence Moran understandably thought of the police as dedicated to maligning and harassing her husband.

After that, it had been a succession of false starts: a paralegal program at Roosevelt University (she lasted two months); training to be a travel agent (she finished the course and worked for two months in the Merchandise Mart, a branch of Ask Mr. Foster); airline stewardess on a feeder line (throughout one windy bitter winter she fluttered between Peoria and Chicago on an old DeHaviland that looked like a waterbug, it stood so high off the runway). And all the time, following Joe and Donna with large envious eyes, probably making novenas that Donna would have a religious vocation. Donna left for St. Louis and, after an interval, Joe turned to her, and Lenore came alive. In the half year before she married Joe, Lenore finally became a real human being. She had never seemed more beautiful and vivacious. They married and, in storybook fashion, seemed to be living happily ever after, settling in Oak Park, having kids. And all along Joe had been pining for Donna. Strange.

He had never liked Joe Cremona. There was something weak about a man who mooned after a girl the way Joe had after Donna. Maybe it seemed worse when the girl was your sister. Randy knew his sisters were beautiful while he had been shortchanged on looks, ending up with the worst traits of both sides of the family, but he had grown up with Donna and Lenore and of course knew sides of them strangers would not. But any woman you marry is somebody's sister. No wonder marriages fall apart as soon as a couple gets to know each other, really know each other. Not that that explained what had happened to Lenore and Joe.

"If he doesn't want to see you, forget the son of a bitch," he advised Lenore when he talked with her in the basement apartment on Walton Street. "He's not going to get out of jail alive anyway, killing a nun."

He had not wanted to think what the reaction would have been if she had been simply Iggie Moran's daughter, not a Carmelite nun, who had been drowned. Lenore looked at him long and silently; it was like being looked at by his father.

"He's my husband."

"Yeah."

"You go see him, Randy. Make sure he's taking his insulin."

She spoke of Joe as if he were a baby. She gave Randy syringes to take to Joe.

"Can he give himself a shot?"

But Lenore gave him a look. "That he can do."

When he offered Joe the use of the apartment, a big mistake, Joe couldn't completely hide his disapproval. Had the guy ever used the apartment before stashing Donna there? Randy would have bet against it, but you weren't supposed to bet on a sure thing. Horace would have let Randy know.

Moriarity wore the usual smart-ass look of a cop when he came into the office.

"Some layout."

"Thanks."

"What exactly are Moran Enterprises?"

"You thinking of investing in the company or what?"

"No, I just wonder what sort of enterprise set you up like this."

"My father left me money."

Moriarity hadn't taken a seat when Randy invited him to, now he sat down as if it were his own idea.

"We've been talking with the manager of the building where your sister was found dead."

Randy said nothing. His effort to ignore what had happened to Donna was more successful than he would have thought. The trick was to think of her as still down in that convent in Missouri, buried away from the world. Nothing had changed. But hearing Moriarity say it like that, matter of fact, the simple truth, shook his defenses.

"Guy named Horace."

"I know him."

"He's been a lot of help."

"In what way?"

"Guy like that sees everyone who comes in and out."

Randy just looked at Moriarity. Horace would see what he'd been told to see. "It sounds like you've been leaning on the man."

"Not really. I myself wonder why he has suddenly decided to develop such a good memory."

"Look, Lieutenant, I admire your work, I want you to find out who did that to my sister, let's stop fooling around. What did Horace tell you?"

"The one face he recognizes is that of Marilyn Derecho's brother. No mistake about it, he's seen him around the building."

Good old Horace. "You gonna arrest him?"

"Is that your suggestion?"

"I suppose you could poison him at home."

"Funny."

"What do you do, add it to the food like saltpeter?"

Moriarity tipped his head. "He shot himself full of the stuff."

"Yeah?"

"He kept the needle he used to take his insulin."

Randy had lost his desire to banter with the cop. The confused pleasure he had felt at learning that that dumbo Horace had cooked up a story about Alan Derecho to tell the cops was gone. All he could think of now was Lenore pressing those syringes on him, full of worry about her diabetic husband, insisting that he take them to him. Had he carried to Joe Cremona the weapon he used to kill himself? What would Lenore say to that?

FIVE

GEORGIE HAD NO interest in discussing the events they covered while they were fresh and he certainly wasn't going to waste time going over last week's news. Any sympathy he had felt for Briggs was long gone. So Linda called Audrey to find the artist was working late. At eight o'clock she went down to the studio, bringing along a six-pack.

"Briggs?"

Linda nodded. "He haunts me." And she resented more than ever that it was Donna Moran and now Joe Cremona who got all the attention. Briggs might never have existed.

"He left a merry widow, don't forget that." Audrey pushed away from her board to get perspective on what she was drawing.

"Was he in drugs?"

Their eyes met over the board. Audrey nodded. "Just a courier, he said, and I believed him. Money. He had nothing to do with the stuff itself."

"Have you?"

She didn't look up. "Pot. When I was a kid. I'm like Briggs. I prefer alcohol."

Briggs had brought money in from St. Louis twice a month, that's all Audrey knew. Linda thought of the shoulder bag Briggs had clung to.

"Why did he tell you?"

"Pillow talk."

Linda quashed her resentment. It was bad enough to be haunted by the memory of a fat little salesman, she wasn't going to be jealous as well. But there was more.

"I saw him that day, Linda. The day he was killed."

"Where!"

"Here. He looked in to say hello. He wasn't here for a minute. Said he'd call later. Just cut through and went out the back."

"He was supposed to have lunch with me."

"I know."

"He came all the way down here just to say hello?"

"He'd been across the way."

Linda sipped her beer. Thoughts tried to connect in her mind, puzzle pieces that would not fit. Across the way was Alan Derecho. It was Derecho Briggs came to see twice a month.

"Did Briggs have his shoulder bag when he looked in?"

Audrey made a face. "His shoulder bag?"

"Every time I saw him he was hanging on to it for dear life."

Audrey wasn't sure.

"What time was it when he came by?"

"Midmorning."

"After ten?"

"I don't get in much before ten."

"After his appointment."

Audrey shrugged. But that had to be it. Briggs had been to see Derecho. The same Derecho who had pulled a gun on

Katherine Senski when she surprised him in his office. And Briggs had been shot.

"You're not going?" Audrey said, when Linda stood.

"I want to take a look at that boutique."

"They're closed."

"Is there a back door?"

There was. Audrey came with her, thrilled and nervous, not believing that Linda intended to let herself into Alan Derecho's office at the back of the boutique. The skills she had learned from Georgie proved useful. The lock gave, and Linda put her knee and shoulder against the door and eased it open. Audrey was right behind her.

Darkness is a matter of degree. A street lamp half a block away illumined the office with a pale unreal light. Linda pulled the chair back and slowly pulled open the drawer of the desk. No light got to its contents, but when she felt inside, her hand touched the gun. She took it, closed the door and pushed the chair back in place.

"Let's go."

"Aren't we going to steal any clothes?"

"Come on."

Five minutes had elapsed when they were once again in Audrey's studio.

"What was the point?" Audrey asked.

"This."

And Linda showed her the gun she was willing to bet had been used to kill B. G. Briggs.

"Wow. What are you going to do with it?"

"How'd you like to meet some nuns?"

SIX

A JOURNALIST OFTEN acts on premises weaker than those that convinced Katherine Senski Alan Derecho had shot poor B. G. Briggs to death. Both Alan and Briggs were in women's fashions and the link was F. X. Nicolo. The garment salesman had been shot five times, six actually, one wild shot having shattered the window of a parked car. Katherine would not pretend to be able to link persuasively Briggs and Linda and dresses and the boutique and her own fright when Derecho held the gun with trembling hands and might so easily have killed her too, but nonetheless she found a pattern in them.

"How do you plan to put your intuition to the test, Katherine?"

"You mock me, Sister Mary Teresa.

"Not at all. I know you would not lightly entertain such a suspicion."

They heard the sound of female voices long before Linda appeared in the doorway, followed by an extremely tall young woman.

"This is Audrey," Linda announced, and she might have been producing a rabbit from her hat.

Emtee Dempsey was delighted to see Linda and her tall companion, and of course Katherine could not leave now. They adjourned to the living room, where Kim was instructed to take orders for refreshment. Katherine asked for sherry and the other two guests followed suit, though without enthusiasm. Emtee Dempsey had nothing, she never did. She would rather dehydrate than make frequent trips from her desk and her capacity to go without liquids was camel-like.

"We know who killed Briggs," Linda said, not even sipping her drink first.

Emtee Dempsey glanced at Katherine. "Alan Derecho?"

"How did you know!"

"Katherine Senski has been explaining it to me."

Katherine broke in. "What makes you think he killed Briggs?"

For an answer, Linda turned to Audrey. The artist drew from a colorful sack a gun, holding it by the barrel. She extended it so that all could see.

"This is the gun with which he shot Briggs."

Katherine felt at once vindicated and upstaged. "How did you get hold of that?"

They were like two teenagers at a pajama party recounting an exciting experience, sharing the story.

"I've seen you before," Audrey said to Katherine Senski.

"She went to see Alan Derecho," Linda said, and Audrey nodded.

"Of course. That's where it was. The Poops."

Katherine and the old nun exchanged a look.

"I've seen you before too," Audrey said to Kim Moriarity. "You've been to the boutique too."

"Now that we're all acquainted, perhaps you two will give me a coherent account of what you've been up to."

The old nun listened with impassive expression to the scenario Linda put before her. Audrey had seen Briggs on the very day he had been killed. His ten o'clock appointment must have been with Alan Derecho. But why would Derecho kill a man who apparently was in his employ?

"I think it was his shoulder bag."

"Explain."

Linda explained that every time she had seen Briggs he had been hanging on to a shoulder bag for dear life. It had not been found with his body. It was not among the bags found at the Stevenson.

"Sister Kimberly," Emtee Dempsey said, "I think you should call Richard."

Audrey looked around. "Who's Richard?"

"The police," Linda explained.

"You're turning us in?"

Emtee Dempsey smiled. "Hardly. If you have broken any laws, I don't want to hear of it. But that gun is real enough and I'm sure you want to give it to the police.

SEVEN

R ICHARD WAS FURIOUS. He stood before the fireplace
and glared around the room. The gun was now in a
plastic bag from Joyce's kitchen. His fury had increased
at the suggestion that Sister Mary Teresa had nothing to
do with the confiscation of Alan Derecho's gun.

"Your visitors just showed up on your doorstep with a
revolver that happens to belong to Derecho."

"They came intentionally," Emtee Dempsey said, her tone
dangerously close to teasing. "But their arrival was indeed a
surprise. To say nothing of what they brought. Katherine had
just been telling me of her firm conviction that Alan Derecho
had shot B. G. Briggs."

Richard turned to Katherine, smiling wickedly. "So you
were in on it."

"Richard, will you please tell us why you are so upset,"
Emtee Dempsey said in a no-nonsense way. "These young
ladies have provided you with what may very well be a murder
weapon—"

"Supplied me! They brought the damned thing to you!"

"On their way to turning it over to the police. I suggested we phone you. Now stop this posturing."

Richard glared at her for a moment then burst out laughing. "You're right. Of course you're right. I should be grateful for this valuable piece of evidence, particularly since it's covered with the fingerprints of these young ladies."

"Don't be sarcastic."

Richard ignored Linda. "A good deal of taxpayer's money was wasted as we searched his apartment and office for this gun, but what's that against your generosity in handing it over?"

"His office?" Linda asked.

"Where you found this," Richard said sweetly.

Emtee Dempsey wanted to know what had led the police to search the quarters of Alan Derecho.

Katherine still held her empty sherry glass which, it belatedly occurred to Kim, was an indication she would like more. But she was going to have to wait. This was Richard's moment.

"I have a witness who can place Alan Derecho at the apartment when Donna Moran was killed."

That Alan Derecho should explain both the killing of Donna Moran and that of B. G. Briggs came as such a surprise that the next ten minutes in the living room of the house on Walton Street rivaled the Tower of Babel. Richard, having made his point, about-faced and became as excited as the rest of them. Katherine beamed, her intuition vindicated. Linda and Audrey would have been satisfied to find the one who killed B. G. Briggs but found it quite unsurprising that anyone who could kill that harmless salesman from St. Louis might kill others as well.

"Harmless salesman," Emtee Dempsey murmured.

Kim went for the sherry then and when she returned she was struck by Sister Mary Teresa's pensive manner. She did not join in the triumphant chatter. Jealous? Kim smiled. There were times when the wise old nun could exhibit the traits of a child.

"More sherry, Katherine?"

"My cup runneth over." But she extended it anyway.

EIGHT

WILEY ORDERED A club sandwich and a light beer and ate as if he wished he were back in his office. The prosecutor had a narrow face and knifelike nose and eyes that blinked as if he were sending signals at sea. Did he dream of fame, of a bright public future, eventually a seat in congress? Age mocks the dreams that make the world go round. No, not mockery. But Benjamin Rush, who had known more than his share of success, knew how dissatisfying success can be. He wished Wiley well. And it looked as if he had reason to be confident that he was about to accomplish what he had quixotically set out to achieve under the promptings of Joe Cremona. What Wiley wanted was acclaim. Nailing Iggie Moran had been only a means to that. If he got a conviction of Alan Derecho for the death of Donna Moran, he would be the toast of the town without a doubt. As he bit into a wedge of his sandwich, Wiley looked around the Cliff Dwellers' dining room.

"How long you been a member here, Mr. Rush?" he asked, with his mouth full.

"A long time." He had been younger than Wiley, proposed by his uncle. "Tell me about Derecho."

●

The morning editions had been full of the news of Derecho's arrest on suspicion of the murder of B. G. Briggs. Twenty-four hours ago Benjamin Rush would have had to think before he remembered who Briggs was—the dress salesman from St. Louis who had become accidentally involved in the arrival of Donna Moran, appearing on Cable News as the reluctant interviewee of Linda Pastorini. Sister Mary Teresa had insisted that Rush knew all about the man, but she was wrong.

"My senility is not so advanced that I don't know what I remember."

"Then you're not remembering all you know."

"What do I know about Briggs?"

What he learned was that the fellow had asked Linda Pastorini to lunch, she had accepted and was awaiting his arrival at the Palmer House when he was killed. Shot.

And now at lunch in his club with Wiley he listened to the prosecutor tell of the help the good nuns on Walton Street had been in leading the police and prosecutor to Derecho.

"Not that attention wasn't already turning Derecho's way," Wiley said, inspecting his goblet. Would he turn over a plate to discover its manufacturer?

"Oh?"

"It came down to Randy Moran or Alan Derecho. There weren't any other suspects."

"But you had thought it was Randy Moran?"

Wiley frowned, then hunched forward toward Rush. "Look, I was proceeding on a sound basis."

"Mr. Wiley," Rush said soothingly. "I am not criticizing you."

SIX

THE POLICE LEFT it vague as to how they had come into possession of the weapon that had shot B. G. Briggs, and that was all right with Linda Pastorini. But she felt she had paid a debt to the little salesman from St. Louis by assuring that his murderer would be brought to justice. "Being brought to justice" in Derecho's case meant being arraigned before Agatha Goode who seemed to think the prosecutor and police were the bad guys and the accused a kind of ward of the court, to be protected by her from the insolence of office. Les Allegro the anchor told Linda to stick with the story.

Within days that story had grown far bigger than anyone had dreamed. Motivation for killing Briggs took a backseat to the ballistic report that linked Derecho's gun to the ruthless slaying of the little salesman (however tainted the manner of acquiring the weapon). But even before that link had been established the question Why was answered. A stash of cocaine at the address across from Audrey's had been discovered, as well as a bag full of cash, a bag bearing the initials BGB. The questioning of Derecho began in earnest. There seemed no escaping the fact that Briggs had been a courier as well as a representative of F. X. Nicolo Creations.

"Derecho admits that?" Linda asked Richard Moriarity.

"He won't even admit his name."

"Let me interview him."

"That's up to him and his lawyer."

Derecho's lawyer, Fuller, thought about it when Linda put the question to him. He was at once intrigued and wary.

"The police have been attributing statements to Derecho. Why not let him get his own story out."

"For television?"

"For Cable News. An exclusive."

"Only if I get veto power over the tape."

"Not a chance. Look, Fuller, I'm offering to do you a favor. If your client is going to be tried in the media, why not defend him there?"

Fuller agreed only when he convinced himself he was doing himself not Linda a favor. Derecho was being held in the same cell block in which Joe Cremona had died. He lay in apparent contentment on the Spartan bed, arms folded beneath his head. He looked at Linda from the corner of his eye.

"Have they issued you any poison?"

"The food is lethal enough."

"You seem in good spirits."

"I'm innocent."

"Of what?"

He sat on the edge of the cot. "What am I in here for?"

"The police are calling you a top cocaine dealer. They found a fortune of the stuff in your place of business."

"They had lots of time to plant it there."

"Why would they do that?"

"Because they know I didn't kill B. G. Briggs."

Behind her, Georgie changed positions but kept the camera running.

"Briggs's bag was found in your office."

"I don't know anything about it."

"Is that your story, that you've been falsely accused of one crime and now the police are planting evidence to get you for another?"

"It sure looks that way, doesn't it?"

"Briggs worked for you, didn't he?"

"You bet he did. A great salesman."

"How did he happen to get shot with a gun that belongs to you?"

"That's the most surprising thing of all."

Derecho shook his head and adopted an unconvincing air of shocked naiveté. "Who will it be next? Did you read of the two grandmas who got caught trying to smuggle drugs in from Mexico?"

Being in jail had conferred an uncharacteristic insouciance on Derecho. His denials were at once unconvincing and plausible. By the time his case came to trial, Derecho would have his story down so pat a jury might believe him. Linda had wanted the interview to put a noose around the neck of B. G. Briggs's killer, but it ended by doing what she had told Fuller it would, gain points for his client.

The interview was interrupted when Fuller arrived to escort his client from jail, bail having been unexpectedly set. Did Derecho imagine it would always be this easy to get out of trouble?

"What about your gun?" Linda asked.

Derecho, about to saunter off with Fuller, turned and for the first time looked Linda in the eye. "That's right. My gun."

"This lady turned it in," Fuller said disgustedly. Had he just learned this?

"You?" Derecho looked as if she had betrayed him.

"That gun killed Briggs."

"Where did you find it?"

In the cold scrutiny of Alan Derecho's eyes, Linda realized the dangers of becoming a participant in the news of the day.

"It was in your desk."

"Amazing," Derecho said. "You broke into my office and found a gun. What night was that?"

Linda told him, unnerved by the bright smile that broke out over his face, turning a sinister man into a handsome and engaging one. Fuller too was smiling.

"Mr. Derecho reported that gun missing weeks ago," Fuller said. His smile was genuine enough.

Derecho's brows rose. "You might have to explain who paid you to return it, after it had been used on Briggs."

The lawyer walked away with his client then, and it was a moment before Linda realized she was standing there with her mouth open. Georgie snapped her out of it.

"A likely story," the little photographer said, and Linda realized he was trying to cheer her up.

"Either he did or he didn't."

"Right."

●

Because Randy Moran had offered to be a prosecution witness against Derecho their producer, Zeke Toggle, sent Linda and Georgie on to interview the scion of the Moran family. Randy was happy to accommodate the press.

"His father tried to get mine into the drug racket and he tried to get me involved." Randy tucked in his chin, what there was of it, and looked at Linda over his half-glasses. "I made a point of keeping tabs on him. He had no secrets from me."

"Why?"

"He thought it was only a matter of time before I decided to get some of that big money."

"Did you know Briggs?"

"Briggs."

It angered her that the little salesman was so easily forgotten. It frightened her too. How spooky to think that days after we're gone nobody even remembers us. She reminded Randy who B. G. Briggs was.

"Oh, the courier."

"Why do you call him that?"

"That's what he was. Not that he knew it. That's my guess anyway. He brought the cash in from St. Louis, but he might not have known what it was."

Linda wasn't sure whether or not that was favorable to the memory of Briggs. It turned out not to matter. When Briggs's will was probated in St. Louis everyone including his wife was astonished to find how rich he was. 'Multimillionaire' was the term used. No one believed he had made that kind of money selling women's dresses.

Linda went on to Walton Street, hoping to get an interview with Lenore but was not really surprised when it was refused. By Emtee Dempsey. The old nun just shook her head.

"What on earth would be the point of it, Linda?"

"What's the point of any news?"

"Good question, my dear, good question."

"I've interviewed Alan Derecho and Randy Moran."

"I watched you on the television with a great deal of interest."

"So the news does have a point?"

"Up to a point, perhaps. If one could believe Randolph Moran, he is pure as the driven snow, resisting the blandishments of the wicked Alan Derecho. It makes for good drama."

Linda winced. "The point of the program had been to present the case against Derecho. Chances are that Randy's a far bigger crook, but so far as anyone knows he hasn't killed anyone. Derecho has. He killed Briggs and Donna Moran and—"

"And Joseph Cremona?"

"It looks like it."

"Why?"

"Randy thinks Derecho saw Cremona when he went to the apartment and figured Cremona would remember and decide to let the one who killed Donna pay the price."

"Randy said that?"

"Words to that effect."

"Alan Derecho seems quite unconcerned by these accusations."

Why shouldn't he? His gun had indeed been reported missing and the date on the report was the day before the plane from St. Louis carrying Briggs and Sister Mary Magdalene Moran had arrived in Chicago.

Eventually, however, Alan's other salesmen were tracked down, and while they all claimed ignorance of the contents of the suitcases and shoulder bags they brought to Chicago regularly, there was no escaping the fact that Alan had made drugs the central activity of the family company. Nonetheless Wiley intended to prosecute him first for the murders of Donna Moran and of Briggs.

"Why did he kill Briggs?" Audrey asked.

The suggestion Linda hated was that he had killed Briggs in an effort to implicate the Morans. Despite the wife in St. Louis and the surprising wealth, Linda did not like to think of the fat little salesman simply as a ploy in the schemes of others.

E MTEE DEMPSEY HADN'T wanted Linda Pastorini talking to Lenore, but Randy was another matter. Kim called the brother and invited him to Walton Street.

"What's up?"

"Sister Mary Teresa would like to talk to you. About your sister and her family."

Randy was silent for a moment. "Getting a little tired of your house guests? Okay, I'll be there."

But when Randy arrived, Katherine too was there, and Emtee Dempsey had Kim bring him to the study rather than to the basement apartment. He seemed less than pleased to see his father's old nemesis there but was placated by Katherine's remark that he and his family had come unscathed through recent events.

"Except for poor Donna, of course."

"Joe Cremona was a nut," Randy said, shaking away the ashtray Emtee Dempsey offered him. She had seen him smoking a cigar during the interview with Linda Pastorini and seemed determined to put him at ease. Kim was relieved that the house would not be filled with the reek of cigar smoke.

"The police think Alan Derecho is responsible for your sister's death," Emtee Dempsey said.

"She wouldn't have been in Chicago if it hadn't been for Joe."

"But you think Alan Derecho killed her?"

"I'm not going to tell the police their business," he said expansively.

"They also thought he shot poor Mr. Briggs."

"Yeah." Randy shook his head in sad amazement at the turpitude of men.

"Of course they've changed their minds about that. It seems that Alan had reported missing the very gun used in the killings some days before they occurred."

"If the police believe that, they'll believe anything."

"Oh, it's a matter of record," Katherine said.

"But we know that he still had the gun," Emtee Dempsey said.

Randy, having second thoughts, was reaching for the ashtray, but his hand stopped and he waited for Emtee Dempsey to go on.

"He threatened Katherine with the gun during the period it was supposedly missing," the old nun explained.

Randy put the ashtray on the arm of his chair and began to toy with a still-wrapped cigar. "You tell them this?"

"I have."

"They believe you?"

"They don't want to."

Randy ran the now-unwrapped cigar across his mouth, wetting it. He seemed unsure how to react to this information.

"They got him for Donna anyway," he said. "That's the main thing."

"There they have only the thin reed of the caretaker to lean upon," Emtee Dempsey said. "In any case, it is the death of Joe Cremona that seems to me to present the most vexing problems."

"How so?"

"You visited him in his cell, didn't you?"

206

"A couple times." The words were made visible in the smoke Randy exhaled as he got his cigar going. Katherine put a handkerchief to her face, but the old nun seemed totally unconcerned by this polluting of the air of her study.

"What did you bring him?"

"Nothing."

"Oh? Paul Dudley, the officer in charge, says you brought him Coke to his cell."

"Coca-Cola. Sure. He loved the stuff. I got it right out of the machine down there, in case you're thinking I brought it into the cell block."

"Oh, I didn't imagine you put poison in it," Emtee Dempsey said with a little laugh.

"Just wanted to make sure."

"Not at all. I think you put poison in the syringe you brought him."

Kim held her breath as Emtee Dempsey said this. From the moment the old nun had offered their guest an ashtray, Kim had known she was up to something. But this accusation came as a complete surprise.

"He injected it into his system, thinking of course that it was the insulin he required as a diabetic. I understand you're a diabetic too."

"That's the only true thing you've said."

"You take insulin every day?"

Randy moved uneasily in his chair. "Since I was a kid."

"Have you any with you now?"

Randy looked to Katherine and Kim for help. What was he supposed to do with these crazy questions.

"Could I see your cigar case?"

Randy slapped his chest, involuntarily. He had returned his case to his inside jacket pocket after removing the cigar he now smoked with less pleasure than before. Emtee Dempsey stood and extended her hand. But Randy was shaking his head, puffing furiously on his cigar as he did so, filling the room with metallic blue clouds of lethal smoke.

207

"I noticed syringes as well as cigars when you took out that one."

"Okay. I'm diabetic. It's a precaution."

"Did you have that case with you when you visited Joe Cremona in jail?"

Randy had had enough. He got to his feet and crushed his cigar in the tray. "I came to take my sister out of here. Where is she?"

"Sister Kimberley?"

Kim hesitated, not knowing what the old nun expected. Sister Mary Teresa frowned at her with displeasure.

"Would you ask Sister Joyce to bring our guest here?"

But Joyce was not in the kitchen, and when Kim went downstairs to the basement apartment, there was no trace of Lenore and her children.

"They must have gone out," Emtee Dempsey said to Randy. "Would you care to wait for their return?"

It looked for a moment as if Randy would do just that, but the prospect of an unspecified prolongation of his stay in the study decided him. "Have her telephone me."

"Of course. But please let me see one of your syringes."

Randy removed the case from his pocket and slapped it into the old nun's hands. "Keep it. You can have the cigars too."

Fifteen minutes later, Kim checked the kitchen to see if Joyce had returned. She heard footsteps on the basement stairs and was surprised to see Emtee Dempsey come slowly up the stairs, huffing and puffing as she did.

"Has Lenore returned?" Kim asked.

Clear blue eyes looked up at her through the circular lenses of her spectacles.

"She's not downstairs."

Kim waited but there was no further explanation.

Later, Joyce told Kim that Emtee Dempsey had given strict instructions that Joyce take Lenore and her kids along when she went shopping.

"You went shopping yesterday."

208

"She wanted lamb chops."

"For whom?"

"For the big dinner," Joyce whispered. "Don't let on you knew."

A thoroughly mystified Kim went upstairs to her room. She had no particular liking for lamb chops. Neither did Emtee Dempsey. What was the old nun up to?

THREE

THE LAMB CHOPS were apparently meant as a treat for Katherine, who along with Mr. Rush joined them for dinner that evening.

"You do not deceive me, Sister Mary Teresa," Mr. Rush said, his manner rendered more convivial by the martini he had had before dinner and the wine he had had during. "I know the purpose of this dinner."

"Oh?"

"You have reason to celebrate, I suppose, if you hold me to my promise."

The old nun's little smile indicated she understood as little of this as Katherine or Joyce or Kim.

"The reward, Sister. Fifty thousand dollars I foolishly promised to anyone who provided information leading to the arrest and prosecution of the kidnapper of Sister Mary Magdalene. I suppose you have as solid a claim on that as anyone."

"I? My dear Mr. Rush, insofar as you offered such a reward, you did it in my name."

"Very well. Then we can celebrate the saving of fifty thousand dollars."

"Aren't you perhaps being premature?"

"Apparently you did not think it necessary to wait until the prosecution actually began before calling us together."

"I do not think that things have been settled satisfactorily at all."

Katherine, never uninhibited and even less so now, dismissed Emtee Dempsey's hesitation as the result of an exaggerated desire for a limpidly clear explanation. She undertook to review the facts.

"It all began with the kidnapping from this house of Sister Mary Magdalene, a deed we know was done by Joseph Cremona. He incarcerated the poor girl in an apartment, apparently thinking that such treatment would lead her to fall in love with him, despite his marriage and her religious vow. Clearly an unstable man. He was thought to be unstable enough to lead police and press to the apartment even though he knew what grisly discovery would be made there. Now we can credit his hysterical surprise and accept it as genuine. He did not kill the woman he loved. Who did? The building superintendent places Alan Derecho at the apartment at the crucial time. Why would Alan Derecho murder a Carmelite nun? Motive enough can be found in the fact that the nun was the daughter of the man who had corrupted his sister, had installed her in that very apartment as his mistress. Marilyn Derecho's death from an overdose of drugs could be laid at Iggie Moran's doorstep."

"If that is true, I certainly had no part in establishing it," the old nun demurred.

"That Alan Derecho was capable of murder is established by the fact that two men died from shots made by his gun."

"Which he reported missing . . ."

Katherine smiled. "Oh, there was indeed a report and it was indeed dated days before the shootings in question. But doubt has been raised as to when precisely it was received. There is reason to suspect that the report was an ex post facto attempt to divert attention from Alan Derecho. And of course he acted in a way to undermine his claim that the gun was missing."

"By aiming it at you?"

"Precisely."

"The very same gun?"

"He does not claim to own two."

"So there it is," Benjamin Rush said. "A masterly summary, if I may say so."

Katherine bowed and the two touched wineglasses.

"Three deaths, one killer," Emtee Dempsey murmured. "But what of Joe Cremona."

"He committed suicide!"

Kim did not blame Katherine and Mr. Rush for their satisfaction with this wrap-up of events, and yet like Emtee Dempsey she found it unlike other occasions when it had been the old nun who had tied all the strings together and there had been nothing further to discuss.

FOUR

L ATER, AFTER NIGHT prayer, Joyce went upstairs and Emtee Dempsey returned to her study but Kim stayed on in the chapel, praying for the repose of the soul of Sister Mary Magdalene. She prayed too for the others who had died violent deaths in recent days, Lenore's husband and the salesman from St. Louis, whose surprising fortune they had discussed with Linda. Sensational memories flooded her mind, and it was difficult to remain recollected. Kim had read Teresa of Avila's account of how difficult she found mental prayer. If the saints found it difficult why should she be surprised that she did?

Sister Mary Magdalene had been a Carmelite, like Teresa of Avila. It was something they might have talked about, if there had been any time. Kim thought of the strange little creature she and Joyce had picked up at the airport and driven back to the house. There hadn't been much in the way of conversation during the drive, and at the house the Carmelite had difficulty staying awake in Emtee Dempsey's study. In the morning, they had all gone off to Mass, leaving their guest alone, not wanting to risk having her recognized outside the house. They never saw her alive again. No wonder Emtee Dempsey blamed herself for the cheery way she had assured Donna's superior that the young nun would be perfectly safe here in the house on Walton Street. And she had believed it. Why wouldn't she? How could she have known of an old boyfriend whose passion would lead him to kill Donna rather than let her return to the convent.

Kim's prayers were for the living too. For poor Lenore, who had been told by her husband that he had never loved her, that their children meant nothing to him, that he had married her only to spite her sister who had left him for a religious vocation.

Her mind was still full of these thoughts when she went to the study. She entered and sat, but minutes went by before Emtee Dempsey looked at her.

"Good heavens, Sister Kimberly, you startled me. How long have you been there?"

"Sister, you mustn't blame yourself for what's happened."

"You think I do?"

"You mustn't brood about it."

"I never brood, Sister Kimberly. I would consider myself deficient in trust in God's providence should I give myself up to brooding. Nonsense. I have been reviewing the events of the past weeks."

The phone rang, and uncharacteristically, Emtee Dempsey answered it. It was Dr. Farber the coroner! The old nun did more listening than speaking, and her great headdress swayed as she nodded at what the coroner was telling her.

"What was that all about?" Kim asked when Emtee Dempsey had hung up.

"Dr. Farber was returning my call. Do you suppose Lenore is still up?"

"Sister, it's nearly midnight!"

"I suppose you're right. Well, it can wait until morning."

"What?"

"I have just discovered how Lenore killed her husband."

214

"Lenore? You're not serious!"

"Sister, review with me certain events."

Kim stood staring at Sister Mary Teresa, who pushed aside Randy Moran's cigar case and spread some pages before her. On them was a precise horarium of the days since they had picked up Sister Mary Magdalene at O'Hare. Kim slumped into a chair, wishing she had gone to bed without stopping by the study. Reluctantly she went over the days.

Finally she looked up, puzzled. "But this only proves Lenore never saw him."

"But that did not prevent her avenging herself on her sister and faithless husband. And she used her brother as her agent."

When she finally did go upstairs to her room Kim was unable to fall asleep. It was half an hour later that Sister Mary Teresa made her slow ascent. Would the old nun be able to sleep, now that she believed they harbored in the basement apartment a woman who had murdered her husband by proxy?

5
FIVE

"S HE NEVER GOT in to see him," was Richard's first response when he joined them for breakfast the following morning. "Where is she, by the way?" His voice dropped.

"I thought you were to make certain arrangements concerning her."

"I did. Is she out of the house?"

"Yes."

"Okay. So tell me how she killed her husband when she couldn't get near him?"

"She used her brother. Under the guise of concern for her diabetic husband, she persuaded her diabetic brother to take syringes to the jail, which she had filled with a lethal liquid."

"The lethal liquid was the toilet cleaner at the jail."

"Oh, would that it were! Although it seemed a strange request, I prayed that was the case. Unfortunately it is not. The syringe was indeed filled with such a cleaner, but from a container that will be found in our basement apartment. Dr. Farber was kind enough to establish that his earlier surmise— that the cleaner containing hydrochloric acid was the one in the jail rest room—is unfounded. The proximity of syringe and poison invited that thought, despite the difficulties presented by the fact that Joseph Cremona was not allowed to use the rest room in which the cleaner is found. The suggestion that there had been an intermediary among the inmates proved a futile one. And then we learned that Randy Moran had acted as messenger for Lenore, taking syringes to his brother-in-law.

"Syringes?" He emphasized the plural.

Emtee Dempsey opened Randy's cigar case. There were two cigars and one syringe left. "We must ask Randy why he gave Joe only one. If he had given all, this whole matter could have been cleared up long ago."

"How so?"

"One sufficed to kill him. The others would have been discovered."

"Others?"

"I sent one over to Dr. Farber with Sister Joyce last night. It enabled him to establish that the contents were of a different brand of cleaner than that found in the jail."

"But what if Randy had used one of them?"

The great headdress dipped and rose. "Yes. Do you suppose that was part of the plan?"

"Her own brother?"

The old nun looked stern. "She had already killed her sister, an unnatural as well as a sacrilegious act."

"There is no way she could have killed the nun," Richard said. "The doors of that apartment have deadbolt locks. That's why the nun couldn't escape. And she couldn't have admitted her sister." Richard wore a pardonably triumphant smile. "How you gonna get out of that locked room mystery?"

From beneath her wimple Sister Mary Teresa brought out her watch. She detached a key from the chain and handed it to Richard. "I found this downstairs."

That key did indeed prove to open the locks of the apartment. Lenore's husband had had a key. He still had it when he admitted the police to the apartment on the day the drowned Carmelite was discovered. Lenore, it seemed, had had a copy made when there was talk of Donna returning to Chicago.

She was willing to tell everything eventually, after she had decided to take pride in the awful deeds she had done. She declined the suggestion that Emtee Dempsey come visit her and the old nun's disappointment seemed at least in part explained by her disappointment at not getting inside prison.

"She cheerfully admits to drowning her sister," Katherine reported to the nuns on Walton Street.

Emtee Dempsey was less interested in this than in the state of Lenore Cremona's soul. Every day in their little chapel they prayed for the repose of the souls of Lenore's victims. They also prayed that Lenore would repent of her sins. It was always particularly poignant when they prayed for the two little girls. Randy had claimed his nieces and was taking care of their upbringing.

"What will become of them, raised by an uncle like that?" Joyce wanted to know.

"Perhaps one or both will have a religious vocation."

"To the Carmelites?"

"I was thinking of the Order of Martha and Mary."

"You always are."

The old nun nodded, pleased. "It is a special grace."